A tiny curl of enjoyment broke loose in Emily's stomach. She'd never tried to explain the power of scent before—at least not to someone as resistant as Gil Sorrent.

"You're not gonna put anything on me, are you?" He gave her a look as if to suggest that contact with hand cream might melt the skin off his bones.

"If you close your eyes, you'll find it easier to concentrate on your sense of smell."

He stared at her, then closed his eyes, only to pop them open a second later.

"Keep those shut." Emily put her hand on his shoulder and the contact did something to her she wasn't ready to admit. "Smell this."

He took a moment, searching for the scent. "Um...nuts?"

Emily smiled. "Almonds. See? You're good at this."

"Don't let that get out," he said, opening his eyes. She suddenly realized they were way too close for comfort. He did, too—she could tell by the way he shot up off the stool. "I'm pretty much a no-frills kind of guy, Emily, and I'd like to keep it that way."

Books by Allie Pleiter

Love Inspired

My So-Called Love Life
The Perfect Blend
Bluegrass Hero

Steeple Hill Books

Bad Heiress Day
Queen Esther & the Second Graders of Doom

Love Inspired Historical

Masked by Moonlight

ALLIE PLEITER

Enthusiastic but slightly untidy mother of two, Allie Pleiter writes both fiction and nonfiction. An avid knitter and nonreformed chocoholic, she spends her days writing books, drinking coffee and finding new ways to avoid housework. Allie grew up in Connecticut, holds a BS in Speech from Northwestern University, and spent fifteen years in the field of professional fund-raising. She lives with her husband, children and a Havanese dog named Bella in the suburbs of Chicago, Illinois.

Bluegrass Hero
Allie Pleiter

Steeple
Hill®

Published by Steeple Hill Books™

STEEPLE HILL BOOKS

Steeple
Hill®

ISBN-13: 978-0-373-87494-1
ISBN-10:   0-373-87494-4

BLUEGRASS HERO

Copyright © 2008 by Alyse Stanko Pleiter

This is a work of fiction. Names, characters, places and incidents are either the product of the author's imagination or are used fictitiously, and any resemblance to actual persons, living or dead, business establishments, events or locales is entirely coincidental.

This edition published by arrangement with Steeple Hill Books.

® and TM are trademarks of Steeple Hill Books, used under license. Trademarks indicated with ® are registered in the United States Patent and Trademark Office, the Canadian Trade Marks Office and in other countries.

www.SteepleHill.com

Printed in U.S.A.

But the fruit of the Spirit is love, joy, peace, patience, kindness, goodness, faithfulness, gentleness and self-control.
—*Galatians* 5:22–23

To Savannah, because she loves horses

Acknowledgments

Middleburg gets ALL of its charm—and NONE of its faults—from a lovely little Kentucky town called Midway that immediately captured my heart. Kathy Werking at Soapwerks in Midway was a willing and creative soap resource for me, and Ginny Smith, Connie Camden, the Quirk Café, the Flag Fork Herb Farm and many others showcased the region's warm hospitality. Normandy Farm gave me the inspiration (including the china cats) for Gil's Homestretch Farm, and many of the Homestretch concepts come from a similar program at Kentucky Horse Park.

Thanks—as always—to friends, family, Spencerhill Associates and Steeple Hill Books for walking through this challenging process beside me. Some books come to life easily. Others…well, that's what friends and colleagues are for, aren't they? And God? Well, He's always got the higher plan in mind—count on it.

Chapter One

"How do you reckon anybody breathes in here?"

The drawling baritone from the front door of Emily Montague's bath shop surprised her. She drew in a breath—a very pleasured, scent-filled breath, thank you very much—and looked up at the two men. Outside of Valentine's Day or Mother's Day, men rarely ventured into West of Paris with all its feminine décor and lavishly scented soaps. Certainly not at the end of January.

Certainly not Gil Sorrent.

Sorrent's companion nudged him as they shook the sleet off their jackets. The wet snow barely missed the oiled silk tablecloth on the table near the door. Emily had locked horns with Gil Sorrent enough times to be astounded that he'd even set foot in her shop. He was a big man with big ideas she didn't always like.

Putting on her "customer voice"—the soft, smooth, *How may I help you?* voice—Emily approached the pair. They looked embarrassed even to be in the shop. The shorter one must be new-girlfriend gift shopping. *Time to guide this man to a wise purchase,* Emily thought to herself. With a little cooperation, she could make sure whoever the girl was didn't end up with a horseman's sorry idea of a feminine gift.

That was part of her role in life. Just last weekend at the Bluegrass Craft Expo, she had directed some misguided teenager away from purple turtle guest soaps for his grandmother and steered him toward a lovely sachet for her bureau drawer. Honestly. Purple turtle soaps for your grandmother. How did men come to such insane conclusions about the women they professed to love?

She smiled at the man. "Can I help you find something?"

Remarkably, it was Sorrent who replied. "I need a birthday present for my niece, and I ain't got time to drive into Lexington." His eyes scanned the room, and he tried to hide his wince. "She said 'no gift cards,' but I'm thinking that might just be the way to go."

"Yeah, picking a gift in here ain't gonna be easy for you, Gil. It's not like you spend a whole lotta time with the concept of soap." The wiry man flashed a goofy grin and elbowed him. Right into the stack of soap dishes. Two of which clattered to the floor and shattered.

"Ethan, you're a big clumsy lout sometimes. That's coming out of your paycheck right after I pay for 'em." Sorrent crouched down and began picking up the shards.

Emily ducked behind the counter for a dustbin. "I've got a gift in mind, Mr. Sorrent. And no need to help with that— I'll take care of it after we get you set."

"Nonsense, Ms. Montague," he said, taking the dustbin from her. "I know enough to clean up my own messes. Or," he continued, nodding to his companion, "the messes of the louts I'm dumb enough to bring along with me. Ethan, how about you go find yourself a cup of coffee some-where? You ain't worth a lick in here, and you'll probably cost me more the longer you stay."

Ethan didn't need any further inducement—with a quick nod, he was out the door as if the store were on fire.

"I've been known to call Ethan a walking tornado, but I can't really blame him when it was me who shattered your soap dishes, now can I?"

Although they'd come down on opposite sides at the last town hall meeting, he seemed to be making a genuine effort to be nice. Emily supposed she had to respect that. "He did nudge you," she offered. "Rather hard."

"Ethan's been shoving me for years. I ought to be able to handle it better by now." He scuffed a wet boot on the shop's hardwood floor, looking all too much like the pro-verbial bull in the proverbial china shop. "How about I just make my niece happy and get out of your way before I break something else?"

"I'll help you find a gift, have it wrapped and send you out the door in ten minutes," Emily replied, an idea popping into her head. "I've got some bubble bath the high-school girls just moon over, and I'll add a loofah mitt just to make her extra happy."

"A what mitt?" He raised an eyebrow and followed her carefully to the counter, giving each display as wide a berth as he could manage given his large frame. Emily's shop was intentionally cluttered with all kinds of charming and delicate things. Heaps of crisp linens, vintage tins and settings of white French Market furniture were carefully arranged to intrigue her customers.

Intrigue her female customers, that is. Emily doubted her current customer appreciated the atmosphere.

"Oh, never mind, just put the bubble bath and the other doodad in some teen-friendly basket thing and get me done. And don't forget to charge me for those soap dishes, if that's what they are…were." He tossed a credit card on the counter and stuffed his hands into his jean pockets.

True to her word—as she always was—Emily had his bath basket ready, wrapped and tucked into her store's signature yellow shopping bag in nine minutes. He looked as though it was eight minutes too long, so, on an impulse, Emily tucked two small bars of soap in brown burlap wrappers on top of the lavender tissue. "There's something in there for you and your friend, just to show no hard feelings."

"Something for me? And Ethan?" Now he looked downright suspicious. As if there'd be nothing within four miles of this store that he'd ever consider owning.

She'd been wondering all week what to do with those two extra bars of Lord Edmund's Pirate Soap. A box of twelve—plus the two extra—had been a bonus from an unusual vendor when she bought the full line of their very good soaps. Blythe and Daniel Edmundson were a unique pair by any standards. Daniel was a mop-haired older man with an engaging smile, who loved talking to everyone about his soaps. Blythe, his wife and partner in the business, was a steady, peaceful woman who made you feel as if she'd known you for ages. They looked just like the kind of people who would make purple turtle soaps. She liked to support local artisans and products, even with the dramatic personalities that often came with it. But this Pirate Soap was a bit out of her league. She'd almost tossed the whole box before she'd calculated that the bonus soaps might bring her another fifty dollars in revenue. And every fifty dollars counted these days.

* * *

Gil was turning the corner off Ballad Road when he ran into "Mac" MacCarthy, his longtime friend. Mac ran a civil engineering firm, and together he and Gil had been trying to get some of Mac's improvement ideas in front of the town council. Mac was a whiz at creative solutions on tight budgets, but he and Gil hadn't had much success. Middleburg was far too fond of the way things were to give the concept of change—even change for good or change to keep things from falling apart—much of a hearing.

"What brings you into town?" Gil asked, shaking Mac's hand.

"I could ask the same—can't say I ever thought I'd find Gil Sorrent *shopping* in town." Mac grinned and pointed at the yellow bag.

"Got a birthday thing for my niece this weekend," Gil grunted, wishing he'd stored the bag in his truck before he went off looking for Ethan.

Undaunted, Mac leaned over to inspect the bag. "West of Paris? Isn't that Emily Montague's place? Shopping with the enemy, are we now?"

Gil couldn't really blame Mac for his surprise. Emily Montague had annoyed Gil from the start, with her "don't change this" and "don't tear down that" mentality, keeping Middleburg stuck in the past just to lure more tourists. He'd gotten into more than one argument with her in the past year, the most recent one over the style of Middleburg's street-lights. He rolled his eyes. "I didn't have enough time to run to Lexington. And just because she has outdated ideas about capital improvements doesn't mean she can't figure out what'll make a sixteen-year-old girl happy better'n I can."

"Suddenly you're Mr. Civility? You hated her choice of

streetlight designs. You were the only 'no' vote on the extra appropriations to buy those ridiculous things. Word has it you stomped out after that meeting like she'd shot your dog or something."

Gil tried to cross his arms over his chest, but the frilly yellow bag got in the way. "My dog could have picked a better use for that money. Each one of those lights was an extra four hundred dollars. Do you know how far that money would have gone on our street-resurfacing budget?"

Mac tapped a thick file he was holding. "As a matter of fact, I do. Got the figures right here. I'm on my way over to town hall to try—again—to get 'em on the agenda. Third time's supposed to be the charm, right?"

"I hope so. Sometimes I reckon we're the only sensible souls in this town. Everybody else is so busy being 'quaint' we're in danger of being run down."

"You don't have to tell me." Mac waved the file in the air. "Come on over town hall with me and tell 'em yourself. We'll gang up on them or you can growl until they back down."

"Very funny. I got stuff to do in town while the boys are still back up at the farm. And I got to go fetch Ethan back from the bakery before he cleans 'em out of sticky buns. Call me later and let me know how it turns out."

"Call you in half and hour," Mac said. "Enjoy your bath products in the meantime. Who knew you had a sensitive side?"

I should have driven into Lexington, Gil thought as he headed off down the street, still in possession of that fussy yellow shopping bag. *Anything would be better than this.*

"No. Really?" The older woman buying four jars of lavender bath salts looked astounded.

"Yes, just hours after the concert."

"Bless your heart. That kind of thing just doesn't really happen in places like that, does it? Outside the orchestra hall?"

Emily was surprised at her rendition of the details. She rarely ever talked of her late husband's demise. Most folks in town already knew, and it wasn't the kind of thing that normally came up in conversation with strangers. Even when store chatter strayed over to the very sad tale of Ash Montague's passing, she resisted giving the details. It was hard to watch people react to the story. Good folks balk at an actual murder—murder belongs on television and in spy movies, not in real life. But big crime happens in big cities. Ash thought the orchestra job was a huge opportunity, worth the frequent long trips away from Middleburg. Tuning pianos for a major metropolitan orchestra hall is, after all, a very important job. But sometimes pianos had to be packed up or moved into storage late at night, and things happen. Dark back alleys hide bad people. Lives get…ended.

"Oh," sighed the woman, pursing her scarlet lips and putting her hand to her delicate jaw. "That's beyond dreadful. You poor thing."

"I manage," Emily replied, placing the four bottles, now wrapped in her store's signature lavender tissue, inside the store's butter-colored bag. She tucked a list of next month's sale items inside the bag beside the bath salts. "It's been four years now since Ash's passing." To the day, as a matter of fact. Maybe that's why she'd blurted out the story when the woman had asked if she was married.

"You must miss him, bless your heart. To go in such a…dreadful way."

"Every day." She forced brightness into her smile, not

wanting to end the transaction on a somber note as she pressed the register button. Emily used an old-fashioned ornate brass cash register—the kind that made a delightful *ching* when you pushed the sale button to open the cash drawer. She didn't like computerized cash registers, opting for hand-written receipts instead. Her only nod to technology was the electronic machine that generated credit card sales—and even that was placed in a tiny chintz box so that only the buttons and receipt slot were visible. It wasn't until last year that she began asking for e-mail addresses to send out sale notices, and that was only after the postage rates had gone up again, forcing her to find a more economical way to reach her customers.

"Come back next month when I'll have the matching body lotion on sale."

"I'll do that. I'll certainly do that." Although, from the expression on her face, Emily couldn't quite tell if any subsequent sale would be born out of the quality of her French-milled lavender, or plain old pity for a young Kentucky widow.

She marked down the sale in her tally, lining up the numbers in precise columns. For a bath shop that was supposed to be west of Paris, France, but ended up west of Paris, Kentucky, she was doing okay. Not well, but okay enough to barely make this month's loan payment.

Actually, Emily always made her loan payments, and she always made them on time. Her checkbook balanced down to the last penny every month. Her Christmas cards arrived on time if not early, and her library books were returned ahead of their due dates. She showed up five minutes early for every appointment, and nothing in her fridge was anywhere near its expiration date.

Emily liked to have all her details under control.

So how, she wondered as she stared at her naked left hand and the pale void where her wedding ring had once been, had so much of the big stuff gone wrong?

Chapter Two

The next morning, it was astounding that Gil Sorrent didn't break a *case* of soap dishes when he stormed into the shop. He stalked up to the counter and slammed down plastic bag. "What's *in* there?" he demanded, pointing to the bag. It was a wonder half the store wasn't rocking in his wake.

Emily shot up from her desk by the window. "Pardon?"

Sorrent's voice deepened to the near-growl she remembered from their last town-hall clash. The man had a fierce temper—one she hadn't expected to ignite just by talking about the designs of streetlights. Was it that strange an idea that things should look nice as well as functional? Everyone else on the town council had understood that it would take a few extra dollars to get lights that didn't look as if they belonged on the freeway. He was always going on about improving this or upgrading that—she'd have thought he'd be happy to be purchasing new streetlights for Ballad Road. He didn't look happy then, and he sure didn't look happy now. "I want to know what's in that soap you gave us, and I'm not leaving until you tell me every last ingredient, you hear?"

It took Emily a moment to realize what he was talking about. Then she remembered her spontaneous act yesterday. The Pirate Soap. "Gracious. Did your friend have some kind of allergic reaction? Believe me, I'll do whatever I can—"

"Oh, he had a reaction all right, but it wasn't the itchy kind. Now I mean it, tell me what's in there."

It was at this point that Emily noticed a row of faces pressed up against her shop window—a collection of tough-looking young men, noses flattened on the glass. She panicked for a brief moment, until she realized they were Sorrent's farmhands. Gil Sorrent ran Homestretch Farm, a correctional program for young-adult offenders. Every year he brought on a new batch of troubled young men, usually in their late teens or early twenties, to work the horse farm and put their lives back in order. She'd seen them around town every so often accompanied by Gil or Ethan—the foreman often in charge of the farm's young residents—but they'd never had cause to come into her shop. She'd never met Ethan before yesterday. Awful as it was to say, she didn't mind their absence. They looked…well, they looked *mean*.

But they didn't look that mean at the moment. In fact, they looked downright odd. "Well," she stammered, thinking that Sorrent and "his guys," as he called them, were probably not people you wanted to upset. "I don't make the soap but I can surely find out the ingredients."

"Find out what's in there, and quick." Catching that Emily was glancing over his shoulder, Gil spun around to face the window. The line of rugged faces scattered like mice. She thought she could hear his teeth grind from across the counter.

She looked at the bar, wet and slightly muddy in a plastic bag. "Well, why don't we start by looking at the label." She started to head off to the table where the other Pirate Soap bars were displayed.

"Got it right here." He produced the other bar, still in its label, inside another plastic bag. He held it with two fingers as if it were something nasty he'd found on the floor of his barn. "Ain't nothin' I can see out of the ordinary, but according to Ethan, it ain't no ordinary soap." Red crawled up his neck and threatened to flush his face. He shifted his weight and scratched his chin. He hadn't yet shaved this morning.

"Why would you say that?"

Sorrent shuffled and stole another look at the window. His guys had returned and were now peering into the shop harder than ever.

"Should I tell them to come in?" Emily offered, thinking anything she could do to ease the situation might be a good start.

"Not on your life!" he shot back furiously.

"Okay, well, perhaps you should tell me what happened," she said as calmly as possible. Behind him, one man was pressing an ear to the glass as if to eavesdrop. It was the strangest thing she'd seen in ages.

"Ethan—you remember Ethan from yesterday?" he began, "Well, he's not exactly a ladies' man. Not a fan of clean and shiny, if you know what I mean. But he got caught in a greased chain on the tractor—well, skip the details on that part. Anyways, he got stuck having to use my shower. I tossed him that soap you gave us yesterday cuz I didn't want him griming up my own soap cuz he's filthy and…well, that night…" The man flushed crimson.

"And?" Emily said. "What? Hives? A rash of some sort?"

Gil Sorrent leaned over the counter. "Women. They were all over him like flies on honey. As if he were the last man on earth. And he claims it's the soap." Sorrent lowered his voice even further. "Now, I wasn't there, but you and I both know women do not flock to a man just because of the way he smells, no matter what cologne ads promise. But I had to near wrestle Ethan to get him to give me back that bar. He thinks the soap got him all that attention and those guys out there, they are more than ready to believe him." He pushed the second bar across the counter. "I can't have this kind of thing going on at my farm. So prove to me so's I can prove to Ethan there's nothin' in there to make my foreman such a center of attention."

"Well, of course it couldn't be the soap." She pulled the unused bar from the bag and scanned the rustic packaging. The usual soap and scent ingredients were listed. The wrapper was a vintage style, with a line drawing of ships and waves—nothing to suggest large-scale female attraction would result from use. No enticing claims, no warning, nothing really out of the ordinary except the Bible verse that had drawn her to Edmundson's Soaps in the first place. Every Edmundson soap had a Bible verse on the label.

She pulled open the wrapper.

Sorrent grew still. The young men at the window pressed closer. At the other window on the opposite side of the door, three women now peered inside, curious as to what the fuss was all about.

It was a rather unimpressive little bar—nothing dashing or flashy. Hand-shaped, a bit lumpy and an inconsistent oatmeal-beige color. The Edmundsons probably gave it such a colorful name because it was such a bland-looking soap.

She stared at it, looking for some clue.

He stared at her, agitated.

Because she couldn't think of anything else to do, she sniffed it.

Sorrent held his breath and nearly gripped the counter edge.

She sniffed again. Then a third time. It did smell wonderful. No single ingredient came to mind, but a cascade of scents left her with a single impression of strength, charisma and—though she couldn't explain it—security. It wasn't as though any of these characteristics had a scent. You would never say a man smelled charismatic or secure. Yet, those were the exact words that came to mind when she inhaled. Emily took a small knife from a drawer in her counter and sliced off a corner of the bar. The inside looked the same as the bland outside. No surprises.

She picked the soap back up and inhaled again. It was extraordinarily pleasant, she had to admit. But it was a bar of soap.

She took the corner she'd just cut off and rubbed it against the inside of her wrist. No tingle, no itch, no sudden burning desire to find male company. Well, she was already *in* male company, and he wasn't a hideous-looking man, but…

Emily shook her head, rewrapped the soap and returned it to the plastic bag. "I haven't got an explanation for you."

"I saw your face when you smelled it." Emily blushed and started to defend herself, but Sorrent pointed at her. "It's just *soap,* for crying out loud. You and I both know soap can't *do* that. Make sure no bar of that stuff finds its way back onto my farm. Got it?" Without another word, he turned around and walked out of the shop, the posse of young men scattering to avoid him.

Emily huffed at the door as it swung shut. *Not hideous-looking, but a far cry from good-natured. He can't tell me what to do. He's getting all angry over nothing, besides.* She bent over to toss the cut bar of soap into the trash bin. *The way he's acting, you'd think I'd suddenly become a popular shopping destination for tough-guy farmhands. Honestly.*

When she looked up again, however, Sorrent's guys had scrambled back to her window. After a split-second hesitation, the entire group lurched through her door, nearly knocking each other over to get to her counter first. Emily tried to tell herself there was no cause for alarm, but they were an alarming-looking bunch, all mobbed together like that. And Ethan was nowhere in sight. One was as tall as Gil and twice as heavy, looking as if he could be a bodyguard or a professional wrestler. Another peered at her with squinted eyes, and she could see he was missing a tooth when he smiled—it wasn't exactly the kind of smile anyone would describe as "warm and friendly," either. Another had thick dark hair and spoke with a silky, accented voice. The group contained every version of "tough guy" that Emily could imagine. And this was definitely one of those situations where the whole was scarier than the sum of its parts.

"I'll give you ten dollars for that soap," offered the one with the missing tooth as he pointed to the first wet bar in its plastic bag still on the counter.

"Forget him, I'll give you twenty. You got more?"

"If you can hold it till Wednesday, I'll give you thirty!" a third one cried.

Emily placed her hands over the bar and slid it protectively closer to her side of the counter. The men had been in such a hurry to get to her that the whole lot of them had walked clean past the dozen bars of Pirate Soap on the table behind them.

What in the world is going on here?

Slowly, with all the authority she could muster, she raised her eyes to meet the crowd. "Did you know your boss just told me not to sell you any of this soap?"

A chorus of disappointed moans met her declaration.

"Come on now, ma'am. You don't have to do what *he* says. He's not your boss."

"I could have fifty dollars here by tomorrow morning, lady," offered a small, dark-haired teenager as he pushed his way from the back of the crowd. He had black, beady eyes and a rodent-like grin. "Hey, where else you gonna get fifty dollars for a bar of soap?"

Emily stared at her sudden customers and told herself to remain calm. When she'd asked God to send her a way to make her next loan payment, this wasn't what she'd had in mind. She was thinking more along the lines of a busload of wealthy tourists. Now she found herself holding soap she hadn't ordered with scary-looking men fighting to give her more money than she'd ever made on even her best ladies' soaps.

Maybe she should get another cup of coffee under her belt before she prayed over her to-do list in the mornings.

"Now gentlemen, let's just slow down a minute and—"

"You all better get your sorry backsides out of this shop this instant!" yelled a booming voice from the door. The group turned to find a furious Gil Sorrent stalking toward them. He didn't have to finish the threat. They were scrambling out of the store as fast as they had entered it. The beady-eyed one turned to mouth *Fifty* silently to her, throwing her a wink, besides.

The mob sent the soap-dish table teetering in their wake, and Sorrent was barely able to get his hand under a dish as it toppled off the table. He set it back, muttered something under his breath, gave Emily a quick glare and left the store without so much as a goodbye.

Chapter Three

Soap.

Gil slammed his truck into third gear. Soap is supposed to be home and laundry and Sunday-morning-go-to-churchness. Who knows what they put in it these days? *Fragrance.* That place smelled like a funeral parlor there was so much "fragrance" in it. Made it hard to breathe, much less think clearly enough to survive his last two visits to West of Paris. He'd sent his guys straight home in the van with Ethan and finished up the rest of his errands in a sour mood after his last visit to the shop.

Shop. That's the trouble right there, Gil thought. Give me a *store* every time. A man can trust a store. A store's where you go in, get what you need, pick up a few tidbits and go home with a fair deal. A *shop,* well, a shop's where ladies meander and everything costs too much and you come home with far more than you bargained for. After all, no one goes "storing."

And *everyone* knows what happens when women go "shopping."

Gil had never met a man who "shopped." And he never wanted to.

He hadn't asked for this. He'd never have even set foot in the shop if he weren't so pressed for time. Why hadn't he just gone online and sent something to his niece last week? Now he owned broken soap dishes he'd never use, just because Ethan had knocked him into them. Not that he'd ever be seen with the likes of *those* kind of soap dishes in *his* bathroom. He hadn't picked up the bars of Lord Edmund's Pirate Voodoo Soap or whatever it was called— *she'd* put them in his bag. *Without* his permission. Gil was a man who cleaned up his own messes, but they were usually *his* messes, not catastrophes someone else had created.

"Mud." Gil looked his basset hound straight in one bloodshot eye. "*Never* shop."

Mud swung his enormous head away from Gil and looked out the passenger-side window, as if he found the very word repulsive.

"Good dog."

Gil was leaning over to scratch Mud's ears when his cell phone went off.

"What!" he barked into the phone, still angry.

"Hey, you're the one who told me to call you. Somebody just kick you or something?" Mac's voice was full of humor rather than anger. "So how was your niece's thing last night? Did you smile nicely and play well with the others?"

Gil really wasn't in the mood for Mac's sarcasm. "Enough, Mac."

"Okay, fine. Congratulate me."

Gil blew out a breath. "Congratulations, Mr. Mac-Carthy. Why?"

"We got on the agenda."

"Well, why didn't you say that in the first place? That *is* great news, Mac." Gil's mood changed instantly with the welcome news. Middleburg had been taking the term *rustic* to new heights, and if he and Mac didn't steer their vision toward the future, there wouldn't be much left to visit, no matter how charming. People in Middleburg were fond of the status quo. Very fond. And Emily Montague and her ilk were all too happy to keep it that way. A slot on the next town council agenda was the first step in what was sure to be a long uphill battle to shove Middleburg into the present (much less the future), but Gil was determined to do what he could. "What else is on the docket that night? Anything that could knock us off?"

Gil heard Mac shuffle a few papers. "Civic stuff, some planning for the Character Day speeches at the high school, a couple of scholarship awards and, uh, your favorite folks, the preservation task force. Something about banning ATM machines on Ballad Road. Gotta love that."

"We're done for, Mud," Gil grumbled to the dog as he finished up his call and stuffed his cell phone back in his shirt pocket. "And it ain't even noon yet."

Sandy Burnside pushed through the Middleburg Community Church lobby to find Emily after Sunday service. "Can you do lunch?" she asked, folding the church bulletin and slipping it into her enormous silver handbag. "We've got some stuff to go over for town council. Nice job on the ATM thing, by the way."

"Sure, I'll do lunch, but don't give me all the credit on the ATM. It wasn't that hard to write a letter," Emily countered, waving away the woman's enthusiasm. "How tough can it be to talk the rest of our town council into loving Ballad Road the way it is?"

Ballad Road was part of what made Middleburg so wonderful. It was the kind of main street everyone wished they grew up on—a stretch of unique shops and friendly places to eat where everybody knew everyone else. There wasn't a chain store in sight, everyone decorated to the nines for Christmas and they closed the street down for a festival on the Fourth of July. You didn't run errands on Ballad Road, you visited friends while you just happened to get things done. Sure, it wasn't that big—sometimes Emily had to send customers into Lexington for unusual requests—and it had its share of quirks, but Emily loved every stretch of that eight-block sidewalk. Like the other shopkeepers along Ballad Road, she felt like more of a curator than a merchant. They were protectors of a small-town atmosphere that was almost nonexistent in other parts of the world.

Sandy, even though her clothing shops weren't on Ballad Road, was just as vigilant a soldier in the fight to keep Middleburg's rural charms. Which made her a leader in the fight against Mayor Howard Epson and his ATM machines. "Don't you go and sell yourself short. Howard was near drooling over that dumb idea to put cash machines all over downtown. Must've gotten the idea from some ad in the back of one of his *fi*-nancial—" she rolled her eyes and emphasized the first syllable in *financial* "—magazines. I wouldn't be surprised if he's already made a list of what he's gonna do with his profits. And I'm pretty sure 'tithe it to the Good Lord' ain't on the list."

Emily pulled her jacket from the church's coat rack. "The trouble is you've asked *for* things before. This was just arguing *against* something, even if it was Howard's plan. That's easier—it doesn't cost anything." She looked at Sandy, who was sharp as a tack and probably already knew why they'd met with a bit of success. "Anyone could have figured it out."

Sandy grinned as she reached over and plucked her brown leather coat off a hanger on the other side of the rack. "Not anyone. You. I could learn a thing or two from you."

Funny, I'd always thought it the other way around. Emily looked at her friend as they began the walk into town. Sandy owned three of the largest apparel stores in the county. Though small in stature, Sandy was a bubbly, larger-than-life character. A blizzard of blond hair, bright-pink fingernails and four-inch heels on even her most casual days, you could see Sandy coming a mile off. Sandy had considerable clout in both Middleburg and its city neighbor Lexington, but she never threw her weight around. No, Sandy sort of skipped through life, scattering her influence here and there as if she were a flower girl and life was her own personal, neverending church aisle. If you could dream up a one-woman cheering section, it'd be Sandy.

"You'll be right beside me when we propose that ordinance," Emily reminded her. "I need you and your sparkling personality to keep Howard and his buddies from just looking at the world with dollar signs for eyeballs."

"Nonsense." Sandy narrowed one eye and leaned in close. "They may be prickly, but they smell a skunk quick as everyone else. We don't need to look like a shopping mall to draw folks—Middleburg's best show will always be on four legs."

Emily laughed at Sandy's wild imagery. "Maybe, but

you've always liked the show that walks on two legs and carries a full shopping bag."

"Well, that kind of filly's nice, too. I like our town just the way it is. I say we've always been able to keep 'em pretty and happy and comin' back for more."

And that, Emily thought, was a perfect description of Sandy: Pretty and happy and comin' back for more.

"Speakin' of fillies," Sandy said as they settled into a table at a nearby coffee shop, "I solved your little mystery." Sandy had social connections unachievable by mere mortals. She knew everyone, everyone knew her and Emily had yet to meet anyone who said they didn't like Sandy. Lots of people thought her a bit…much, but they still liked her. If Emily needed anyone to do anything, chances were Sandy knew someone for the job. She was the heartbeat of Middleburg, and quite possibly of the state. "The bit about Ethan Travers," she offered, "and his sudden popularity with the ladies?"

"You did?"

"You're talking about Gil Sorrent's foreman, right? Skinny, bushy hair, kinda wiry lookin'?"

"Yes, that's him."

"Well, women were going after him at the interfaith church social Friday night. If you'd been there, you would have been able to see it for yourself."

Emily, a fan of church but not of church socials, chose to ignore "matchmaker" Sandy's gentle rebuke and keep to the subject at hand. "I know that part, but I need to know why. Ethan doesn't strike me as a real ladies' man."

Sandy started laughing. "No, ma'am, he ain't. It took a little doin', but I have figured out why he was suddenly the center of attention. And I guarantee it don't have a thing to do with soap." Sandy rested her elbow on the table and leaned in. "Doc Walsh's wife told me Thursday afternoon at the Women's Guild meeting that she heard Ethan Travers has a birthmark shaped like the state of Texas on the back of his neck."

Odd as it was, Emily didn't see how it explained things.

"And Barbie Jean Blabbermouth was sitting beside me when she said it."

Now that explained a lot. Barbara Jean Millhouse, aka Barbie Jean Blabbermouth, was so fond of gossip she was practically her own communications monopoly. Anything uttered in Barbara Jean's vicinity was instantly public and often widely exaggerated. Given Barbara Jean's talents, Emily was surprised she hadn't heard that Ethan had a birthmark in the shape of Elvis and that he could make it gyrate on command.

Barbara Jean also had four daughters. Four single daughters, because none of them could keep their mouths shut any better than their mother and far too many Middleburg men had learned that the hard way.

"What did Ethan think? That he'd stumbled onto some kind of love potion? That man's smarter than that. He knows there's no such thing as love soap."

"Actually," Emily corrected, "there is. There's also joy, and peace, and patience, kindness and the rest of the fruits of the spirit—you know, from the passage in Galatians? I just bought a line of soaps from a company called Edmundsons because I thought it was such a clever idea. Edmundsons is also the company that makes Lord Edmund's Pirate Soap, which is what Ethan thinks made him a ladies' man."

"Spiffy marketing. Sounds like just the sort of thing you'd carry in that pretty shop of yours. But mercy, someone needs to set that Ethan straight about what soap can and cannot do."

"Oh, believe you me, I think Gil Sorrent is doing that. In spades. Along with every last one of those guys up on Homestretch Farm."

"Speaking of Sorrent, we're gonna have a hard time convincing him Middleburg doesn't need a herd of ATM machines. Him and his electronic gadgets."

"He'll be a harder sell, but maybe he'll see it our way."

Sandy stirred her coffee. "Let's hope. But Emily, I didn't bring you to lunch just to gab about money machines. I've got somethin' serious to ask you."

Emily looked at her friend. "Everything okay with you?"

"No, not that kind of serious. It's more like somethin' hard. Or you may think it's hard. But a good kind of hard, I'd say."

Emily planted her hands on the table. "Sandy, out with it."

"They were asking for names for the Character Day speech up at the high school. I told them I'd ask you."

"Me? Give a speech at Character Day? That's hero stuff. Not my kind of thing. Why on earth did you tell them you'd ask me?"

Sandy leaned in and took one of Emily's hands. "Because the topic is 'Standing Up for What's Right.' And the quote they're using is the one about how the only thing evil needs to prevail is for good men to do nothin.' And that, sugar, *is* your kind of thing."

Emily pulled back. "No. I'm not ready to do that."

"I wish you wouldn't turn it down so quickly. I think it's time for you to raise your voice. It's not like everybody don't already know what happened to Ash. Most everyone would know why you were there. How many other people have had something tragic like that happen because the one person

around to stop it wouldn't? There ain't nobody in Middleburg with a more powerful story on that subject than you."

"That's just it. Everybody already does know—they
don't need to hear it from me."

"Maybe not, but I think *you* need to say it. How long
has it been now, four years? You've never spoken up. You
hardly ever talk about Ash's murder and how it affected
you. You think we don't see how it hurt you? When they
stopped looking for that one witness, don't you think we
felt it alongside you? There's a whole town waiting to let
you back into life, Emily. But you gotta come out when we
open the door."

"Sandy, no." Emily pushed away her lunch, her
appetite gone.

"Look, I know it'll be hard. I know what I'm askin'. But
I think you'd give such a powerful talk that none of those
kids would ever forget it. And maybe, just maybe, one of 'em
will find themselves in a situation of having to take a stand
like that, and they'll step up because they remember you."
Sandy blinked back a gathering tear. "You know, I can think
of no finer tribute to Ash. He'd've done it if it were him."

"He's not here." Emily fought the lump in her throat.

"So be here for him. And for you." She grabbed both of
Emily's hands. "Just tell me you'll think about. Don't say
no till you've thought about it and prayed about it. Okay?"

Emily gave in. Refusing Sandy Burnside just wasn't
something the average person could do.

Chapter Four

Monday night, Emily spread her two problems out before her on the living-room floor.

On the one side was the stack of three scrapbooks that held clippings from all of Ash's memorial services, obituary notices, newspaper articles and the dozens of cards that had been sent to her after his passing. All the paper accounts made it sound so clean, so clinical. "Search for Known Witness Continues." "Montague Case Closed." "Scholarship Fund Established at Middleburg High." She could scan those with an odd detachment. Keep them contained like the clippings held in place by those little black photo corners. It was the real-life details—the taxi receipt he had in his pocket that night, the box of tuning equipment that she kept in her garage, his shirts that hung in the back of her closet, the wedding ring the funeral director insisted she keep even though she wanted to bury it with Ash—it was those things that always did her in. They wouldn't contain themselves neatly in her scrapbooks. Instead, they spilled out, reminding her how messy her life had felt since Ash's loss. While she'd taken a strange comfort in compiling and organizing the scrapbooks, she couldn't seem to cope with those details. They remained loose ends she couldn't tie off.

Othello, Emily's enormous orange cat, wandered in to inspect the scrapbooks, padding at the corner of one page with a round butterscotch paw. "Do you miss him, Othello?" Emily ran her hand down the cat's smooth back. Othello had been a gift from Ash on their first Valentine's Day as a married couple. She was expecting something big—Ash was an incurable romantic, and she was the envy of many women when he went his usual all-out for Valentine's Day. When he arrived at the house with a single basket, she wasn't sure what to think.

Until the basket said, "Meow."

Ash was a dog person to Emily's cat person. They'd gone round a few times about whether or not they could ever agree on a pet and come to no good compromise. "Otto," as his ratty old collar had identified him, had wandered into the orchestra hall over the weekend while Ash was in the city, and somehow formed an attachment to Ash. No owner could be found during the week Ash was working on the orchestra pianos and the cat persisted in hanging around. The cat just plain wore him down, as Ash always put it. When it came time to head back to Middleburg, it was clear that Otto was coming along. And so it was that Otto became the most loving Valentine Ash had ever given her. It seemed such a grand and romantic gesture that Emily felt Otto deserved a name with more distinction, and Otto became Othello.

He'd wandered the house restlessly for days when Ash died. He'd never done that when Ash was away on trips, but somehow the cat had known Ash was gone for good. It broke Emily's heart to watch Othello sit on the back of the couch and look for Ash's truck to come up the street.

"I miss him, too, boy. I think he'd know what to do about all this."

On the other side of the living-room rug lay problem number two: all of the Edmundson's soaps. It was easier to look at the soaps. They'd stirred up a lot of mess for something that was supposed to clean. The bars weren't even that attractive—unwrapped, they were lumpy, inconsistent rectangles Emily doubted she'd have even noticed on a shop counter if it weren't for their intriguing scents.

Love. Joy. Peace. Patience. Goodness. Gentleness. Faithfulness. Kindness. And self-control. They were all here, all with distinct scents that matched their labels with surprising accuracy. How had the Edmundsons created the scent of patience? She had no idea, but they had. It was the Patience Soap that had caught her eye at the craft expo. Not only because of the scent, but because "patience" was such a curious thing to name a soap.

The other thing about the Edmundsons that drew Emily in was their exuberant faith. No one before that unusual couple could have convinced her that faith could be linked to soap. They were living examples of the Bible verse that talked about doing whatever you do as unto the Lord. To them, it made perfect sense to put their faith into their soap business. Which made it easier for her to embrace putting her faith into her bath-shop business. To Emily, they weren't just vendors, they were inspirations—purple turtle soaps aside, of course.

Emily had jumped at this chance to display her faith in the shop, buying the entire line. It was brilliant that each soap had its own Bible verse printed on the inside of the label. She'd have bought twice as many boxes if she could have afforded it.

But she'd not bought the Pirate Soap. No, the Edmundsons had thrown that box in as a bonus for her big order.

Some gift. That soap was more bother than bonus.

She picked up a bar of Pirate Soap and tried again to figure out its distinctive smell. Citrus, with spice and something botanical like sage or thyme. They had a bit of texture in them, and they were too rough for a woman to use. But *to* a woman, they smelled very…compelling.

Compelling? This from a very articulate woman in the field of scent? Emily was accustomed to identifying and recommending scents easily. To knowing what scent to use where. It bugged her that this Pirate Soap wouldn't sort itself out in her brain, that she couldn't pick out exactly what she smelled and why she liked it. She used scents all the time in her home and at the shop, and she'd been sensitive to them her whole life. Her father had been a real estate broker, and she remembered him putting vanilla extract on the light bulbs in a home for sale, because it gave off the faint aroma of baking. And baking always smelled like home. Scents could calm or enliven. Scents could trigger memory or emotion as easily—perhaps more easily—as words.

But scent did not answer prayers or build character or make Ethan Travers instantly attractive.

So why did someone like Gil Sorrent get all hyped up about it? He *forbade* her to sell the soap to his employees. She found that highly irritating, even if she did somewhat understand his motives. His guys were young, granted, but they were adults capable of making their own decisions.

Even if Gil felt them to be poor ones. These men were eager to be her customers, and unconventional as they were, she didn't think she could afford to refuse their business.

Lord, I need a way to know if I can give that speech. I've also got to find a way sell the soaps but not tick off Gil Sorrent. She sat cross-legged in pajamas on her living-room rug and pondered. She made lists, charts, pro and con tables and generally paced around until at least one of the solutions came to her.

Sell, don't scalp. Of course.

That was the solution: Sell Lord Edmund's Pirate Soap, but don't scalp it. Sell for the same price as all the other Edmundson soaps. If men were rushing into her shop to buy soap, then they would get a fair deal, and the clear explanation that they would get *nothing* from the transaction except *clean.* It was, after all, the easiest antidote to the uproar: Soap that did nothing would kill the rumors about its wonder-working properties. Men liked hard evidence, Ash had always said. Well, she had thirteen bars of hard evidence, and they were going to do their job. Even Barbie Jean Blabbermouth couldn't override good, hard evidence.

Then maybe, she mused, *I can get a few of them to go home with a second bar of some other soap. Herbal hand cleaner, I'll call it.* Emily grabbed her notebook, drew up a plan and packed everything up before going to bed. The soap matter, at least, felt sufficiently resolved.

As for the speech, well, that would have to wait until another day.

Tuesday morning, Emily remembered her pledge to have a second cup of coffee, ensuring she was wide awake before she began her morning tradition of praying over her to-do list. She and God walked through her schedule and her task list, and she asked for help with the challenges of the day. It was an especially nice day for January, clear and crisp with invigorating morning sunshine. Emily opened up a bar of Edmundson's Joy Soap for her own personal use. It had a pleasant, lemony scent cut with verbena and another floral essence she couldn't identify. True to its name, it was a happy soap. A high-quality soap, too. The Edmundsons had achieved a lush, silky soap at a price that suited her shop and her clientele.

"With more sales like that I can save enough to take out an ad next month," she told Othello as she scratched him behind the ears at breakfast. "I bet I can even draw up an annual marketing plan. Love soaps for Valentine's Day. Faithfulness for anniversaries. Kindness soap as a thank you gift. Peace for Christmas. I could put a card in the gift wrap with the verse from Galatians." Othello blinked. "Then, if it works out, I could give a special price for the eight-bar set—it'd make a great confirmation or baptism gift, wouldn't it?" The possibilities spread themselves out before her.

Othello wound his way around her legs and stared up at her with his round yellow eyes. *Sounds brilliant to me,* he seemed to say.

"I'll let you know how my plan works out at dinner, Othello. Maybe we'll have to celebrate a successful day."

This plan really seems brilliant, she thought as she walked to work, enjoying the beautiful day.

And then she turned the corner onto Ballad Road and saw the line. A dozen or so men stood waiting outside West of Paris. Emily's beady-eyed top customer defending his spot at the very front of the bunch.

The Homestretch Farm workers: her newest, unlikeliest patrons. Those young men looked every bit the hard cases she'd heard they were. Some people said every one of them had had a criminal record before his sixteenth birthday. Every spring when the new hands came onto the farm, the town quietly held its breath because they looked like such a crop of miscreants. They seemed to look tougher and meaner every year. Emily was afraid of half of them, quite honestly, even though she felt bad for feeling that way.

She'd been against the farm when it had first opened three years ago. It seemed like far too big a risk for so small a town. However, Sorrent's farm hadn't given Middleburg much trouble. He'd kept it under tight control and even joined the town council. There had been very few complaints.

But that was before this morning. Emily wasn't sure she was ready to get so friendly with Homestretch's questionable residents. *Still,* she told herself as she walked up the street to her shop, *they look no meaner than a banker would look foreclosing on your loan. Smile, and remember how long it's been since you made a dozen sales before eleven.*

She clutched the plan in her basket of work papers and reminded herself she'd come up with a brilliant solution. If she could just stick to it and hold her ground with these men, her problem would be solved before noon and the whole absurd episode of Lord Edmund's Pirate Soap would be over by day's end with nothing but clean men to show for it.

"Good morning, gentlemen," she said as the bodies split into a human hedge leading up to her door.

The Latin-looking one—the one with the silky voice who had winked at her the other day—winked again. "Morning, Miss Montague," he said.

"No work today?" She turned the key in the lock and heard their feet behind her. She wanted to ask, "Does Mr. Sorrent know you're here?" but couldn't bring herself to do it. Of course Sorrent knew they were here. He knew where they were every second of every day.

"We got to be back in half an hour," one of them said. "So we gotta work fast."

"I want two bars!" a lanky boy who barely looked old enough to drive said from the back of the throng.

"Me, too!" cried another. "I'll pay ten a piece."

"Fifteen!" came another shout.

Emily stilled the key and turned to face the crowd. She was glad to count only ten faces—that made things easier. *The plan. Work the plan.*

"Let me make one thing perfectly clear: you'll pay the regular price of four dollars, and I'll sell each of you *one bar* of soap—no more." A chorus of moans rose up from the band of soap-seekers. "And I want you to understand clearly, in no uncertain terms, that these soaps will do nothing but *get you clean.* They're soap, and nothing else, and I'll have a bone to pick with any of you that claims otherwise."

There was a moment of thoughtful silence, and Emily heaved a sigh of relief as she opened up the shop and let them inside. Was it possible that she'd gotten through to them?

"Sure, Ms. Montague," said the oldest of them, "whatever you say."

He must have thought he'd been hiding the smirk on his face, but it became instantly obvious to Emily that they hadn't absorbed a word. They'd still have plunked down twice as much with glee. Well, that couldn't be her problem. She'd come up with her best possible solution—

whether those men learned from it was going to have to be Gil's—or God's—problem.

Emily did, in fact, make her midweek income goal by noon. Suddenly the Homestretch Farm men weren't looking so scary. She was pretty sure, however, that Gil Sorrent would show up sooner or later, and sure enough she was sorting through the noon mail when he skulked through the door. It struck her, as he made his way to the counter, that she'd never seen him happy. Or laughing. She'd seen a smile or two—mostly when he won his point soundly at a town hall meeting—but that didn't really qualify as happy. She couldn't remember having a purely social or remotely chatty conversation with him—all of their encounters could only be described as adversarial. In fact, outside of town council business, she'd hardly ever even seen him at all.

"Had a good morning?" It was barely a question, and it became an accusation when he added, "Taking my guys' money?"

She'd known it was coming, and she had a defense planned. "Now look here, Mr. Sorrent. I don't claim to know how to run your farm, so I'll thank you not to tell me how to run my shop. If those grown men come in here asking for soap, then I'll sell them soap."

He stared at her, a little surprised.

"I've given this a lot of thought," she continued, emboldened by the fact that he hadn't yet jumped down her throat. "I think the best thing for all concerned is for that soap to be in their hands. Disappointing them. I turned down their offers to pay all kinds of wild prices. And I made it mighty clear that the soaps would do nothing but remove grime."

Sorrent swung his weight onto one hip. "And you really think that sunk in?" It wasn't exactly an agreement, but it was better than the tirade she'd expected.

"Well, not yet." His eyes narrowed to near slits but she continued anyway. "But if I'd held those soaps back, it'd be as bad as endorsing the rumor that they do something special. You and I both know they do nothing special, so the best thing for everyone is to get those soaps out, used and gone."

He crossed his arms. "No good can come of this."

"Nonsense. I think just the opposite. By tonight, you'll have the cleanest, most pleasant-smelling farmhands you've ever had. And any and all rumors of Lord Edmund's Pirate Soap and its unique abilities will be dead and gone."

He gave her a look that let her know just what he thought of that prediction. She smiled at him and held her ground. And then he surprised her. "My niece, by the way, went gaga over whatever it was that you picked out for her. Thanks." He didn't quite smile, but his expression edged toward a reluctant pleasantness, if you could call it that.

"You're welcome."

"Which makes me think you're a smart businesswoman, so would you mind telling me what you've got against ATM machines?"

Ah, so he had read her letter to the town council. "I have nothing against automatic teller machines, when they're where they belong."

"And where's that?"

"In banks. Grocery stores. Theme parks. But not on four different Middleburg street corners. Honestly, it's a four-block walk to the one at the bank. Now we've got to have them mounted on the streets like parking meters?"

"People today don't carry cash around. We're in the age

of the debit card, Ms. Montague, and we'd best figure that out sooner rather than later."

"Tell me, do you think people come out here to escape the city, or to see an ATM at every turn? It's the parking meters and ATMs and bustle that they're running *away* from when they come here. They don't want a drive-through with burgers and fries, they want apple pie and coffee. I'm not against technology, Mr. Sorrent. I just don't want to be accosted by it on every street corner."

He turned and looked out the window. "Four is not one on every street corner."

"We're not a big town. Ballad Road's downtown is just a few blocks long. The bank's smack dab in the middle of it. We can't expect the average American consumer to walk four blocks? I don't know about you, but I like to think of my customers as a mite more capable than that."

"It's a convenience thing."

"It's just as much about town atmosphere as it is convenience. And tell me, have you given any thought to who it is that pockets all the service fees for those ugly little machines? And have you seen them? They'd look like giant metallic mushrooms sprung up on our street."

She had him there. "I grant you, they're not very artistic," he agreed, "but they're cash machines, not sculpture."

"Our streetlights are streetlights, but they still look nice and fit the character of our town." Emily crossed her arms over her chest.

Sorrent shifted his weight to the other hip and scratched his chin. "What if there were only two—one at each end of the town farthest from the bank? And what if I talked Howard into putting you in charge of selecting the design and the mounting?"

She was about to let him know that two ATMs was two too many when he held up a finger and added, "And what if twenty-five percent of all the profits went to the town beautification fund?"

Emily fiddled with her register buttons for a moment as Sorrent watched her. She'd lost a sale last week when the couple buying dish towels didn't have enough cash and didn't want to use their credit card. She'd told them where the ATM was, and they said they'd walk down there and come back for the towels, but they never did.

And she'd get to choose the design. Not Howard Epson, who couldn't be counted on to choose red paint for a barn, much less a piece of public structure. And Howard would be forced to donate one quarter of his profits to the beautification fund—the fund that paid the extra money for those particularly lovely streetlights.

Choose your battles, Emily's mother always said. *Know what hill you're willing to die on and why.* Sometimes your goals planned your solution, and sometimes your solution planned your goals.

"Mr. Sorrent, you've got yourself a deal."

Chapter Five

Gil walked through his bunkhouse that afternoon, shaking his head. Of the room's twelve bunks, ten of them had those yellow bags from Emily Montague's shop sitting on or near them.

He sighed. He bought the guys perfectly suitable soap—he bought the guys lots of things, actually. It was part of his long uphill climb to get them to realize they mattered. The first step to making people think they have potential is to treat them as if they have potential. Gil knew that it was up to him to get this idea through to them, and he did, in a thousand small ways over the course of the months he had with them.

Horses were one of the best parts of his program. Teaching the men to treat the horses with kindness and respect was a roundabout way of teaching them to respect themselves. Horses were patient listeners and nonjudgmental companions, so they were a good place to start when learning to care about something. They put up with most small errors but let you know when you'd made a big mistake. One of Gil's first residents had jokingly called the horses "stunt people"—and it wasn't that far off. Lots of days Gil prayed for as much patience and wisdom as his horses had.

A horse would have enough sense to steer clear of Pirate Soap.

Gil walked by Mark's bunk and grimaced at the bar of Pirate Soap he saw lying there. Mark had been one of the hardest cases he'd ever had. King Lear, the horse Mark cared for, had been the first thing bigger than Mark that hadn't beat him up. That tough horse and that tough guy had wrestled themselves into an understanding of each other over the months. Gil hoped all that work wouldn't come undone because of some dumb soap gimmick. As far as he'd come, Mark still kept an eye peeled for the shortcut, the easy out. He had a soft spot for Mark because he saw so much of his former self in the young man.

Not that he could admit to anything openly. Human-to-human caring rarely showed up between these guys—that's what made caring for horses such a good place to begin learning. Healthy relationships were like a foreign language to them: combat, defiance and violence were their mother tongues. So "caring" started with the horses, but eventually Gil added a human element, buying a guy a new T-shirt or his favorite pizza. These became footholds as the men discovered how people cared for each other.

He'd never have paid for their current taste in soap, though. The bunkhouse showers would probably smell worse than Emily Montague's bath shop come sundown. If it wasn't January, he'd have told Ethan to set up dinner outside.

And there was Friday night. That would be a fiasco for

sure. He'd taken them to last Friday's church social in response to a correctional officer's suggestion that they get more social interaction. Oh, they'd got social interaction that night, but he didn't think that was what the County had in mind. He'd bought a block of tickets to the community theater musical for this Friday night. It had seemed a safe enough idea at the time, but he was starting to think that unleashing those guys anywhere near town might be a bad idea. The play was *The Music Man* though, where a good deal of swindling happened, so it might serve as a timely moral lesson.

Gil took one last look around the bunkhouse, thinking he ought to just scoop up the soap and throw it out. Gratifying as it might feel, though, it wouldn't help. He had to respect their decisions if he expected them to respect his. And as much as he hated to consider it, Emily Montague might be right about some lessons only being learned the hard way. Maybe now was the best time to teach them that a woman valued how a man treated her, not how he spiced up the air between them.

He picked up the bag on Larry's bed and sniffed at it. It was awful. Emily Montague'd thought highly enough of it, but she was a woman given to that kind of thing. He'd seen that "pleasant enough" scent do something to her, make her eyes get a funny, faraway look. She'd certainly never looked that way during a council meeting. No, that was a face he never saw across the table at town hall.

Gil hit the power button to open the windows in the farm van as they drove into town Friday night. *This had better be worth it.*

"Hey," came Steve's aggravated voice from the back

row of seats, "the *hair.*" Steve was in his late teens and still growing into his gangly limbs.

"Hey," Gil shot back, "the *air.* My lungs outrank your 'do.' And since when did you care so much about your hair?" At this rate, all of Middleburg would catch the scent of them before they even pulled into the parking lot. When he'd planned on attending the theater tonight, Gil hadn't counted on needing to sit downwind.

Steve made a show of holding down his unruly but now unruly-and-gelled locks. "There'll be women there. They love plays and stuff. Especially musicals." He said the word as if musicals were at the bottom of the theatrical food chain in his opinion.

"Any females present will be watching the stage, Steve, not you. The only one who'll be watching you closely tonight is me."

"I don't think so," came another voice from the back of the van. "That hair's bound to draw stares." A rousing chorus of commentary on Steve's hair rose up from all over the van.

"Settle down, gentlemen, or—"

"—you'll turn this thing around," came the simultaneous response from every seat in the van.

Remind me, Lord, why it is that I do this again? Gil pulled into the high-school parking lot with a sigh. Some days he truly felt as if he was shepherding these young men into maturity. Other days, it felt more like herding hyperactive water buffalo.

And tonight, it was a toss up as to whether you'd smell the water buffalo or the guys first.

If Emily Montague happened to be there, he'd make sure his fragranced little herd sat right next to her. That way she'd get a good whiff of what she'd done.

* * *

As it turned out, the only one sitting near Emily Montague was him. By the time he'd rounded up his "herd" and gotten them into the auditorium, they'd ended up on the far left, split between two rows. Which meant he had guys to the left of him and ahead of him. Gil was on the aisle, with Emily directly across from him in the next section. While such an arrangement granted him a good view of them (not to mention most of them within arm's reach, should they act up), it also gave him a clear shot of Emily for the entire evening.

She was sitting with Janet Bishop, the woman who owned the hardware store, and Dinah Hopkins, the woman who owned the bakery where he took the guys each week. They laughed and chatted in between scenes as if they'd been friends for a while. While Janet had short, dark, practical hair, and Dinah's was a wild red, Emily's hair couldn't seem to decide if it was blond, brown or red—opting instead for a chaotic mixture of all three. It tumbled across her head and down her shoulders in cascades of near-curls that looked too natural to be set, but pretty enough to have been fussed with some. He'd never seen her in a bright color—she always wore pale and pinkish tones that reminded him of Easter.

When he thought about it, her obvious rapture with the play made sense. It was just the sort of nostalgic thing that would appeal to a woman living in a bitty, white, gingerbread cottage that sat like a little frosted cupcake just off Ballad Road. Her window boxes were always full. He suspected all her china matched perfectly. He could see her in the role of Marian the Librarian, even though Audrey Lupine—the woman onstage who actually *was* the Middleburg librarian—was remarkably good. Audrey added to the true-to-life nature of the play already established by the Middleburg High School marching band playing Harold Hill's marching band.

Gil's eyes kept straying to Emily all through the ballad "'Til There Was You." She rested her chin in one hand and let her head fall to one side during the second chorus, even though the leading man didn't have a voice to match Audrey's. She sighed at the song's ending kiss, and he felt it somewhere under his ribs.

At intermission, Gil ventured over to the Arts Guild bake-sale table. After shelling out an unnatural sum to Dinah for a dozen Rice Krispies treats that were big enough to be Rice Krispies bricks, he ran into Emily and Janet at the lemonade pitchers.

"How are the soaps working out—or should I say not working out?" Emily ventured, nodding her head toward the guys.

Janet Bishop smiled. "I heard the story. Your farmhands put in quite an effort tonight."

"I had to roll down the van windows on the way here," he complained, and then realized the rudeness of his insinuation. It was Emily's product, after all. "No offense, of course. I'm sure you gals think they smell great. I'm just not used to my boys smelling like the fragrance counter at a department store."

"I must admit, it does seem like they were…enthusiastic in their use of the soap." A wry smile crept up one corner of Emily's mouth.

"And the hair gel," Janet added. "And a bunch of other…things."

"Tell me about it," Gil replied, taking a swig of lemonade. "I can hardly wait for it to backfire."

The smile left Emily's face as she looked past Gil. "Um…I might have miscalculated on that one."

Gil felt a rock settle into the pit of his stomach. He'd turned his attention from them for five minutes at the most. Now what?

Emily pointed at the guys, now edging their way closer to a group of young ladies—a gaggle of females who, alarmingly, seemed to be edging their way closer to the guys. Outnumbering his guys. Looking interested—sauntering and tucking strands of hair coyly behind their ears. So much for the correctional office's idea of healthy social interaction.

"It's just because they're clean and nicely dressed, that's all," Emily offered.

"Nothing will come of it," Janet said into her lemonade.

Gil crushed the paper cup he was holding and lofted it into a nearby trashcan. "I sure ain't going to let them stick around long enough to find out."

"Aw, come on, intermission ain't over," Marty complained, craning his neck around to get another look at the girls as Gil planted the man in his seat.

"It is for you guys."

"You can't keep us from talking to girls," Mark challenged.

"Watch me. Y'all are practically on the prowl this evening, and I'll have none of it." Gil pointed at empty seats until one by one, the guys sank into them. That still didn't stop a few from turning in their seats to wave and smile.

"Aw, Gil, where's your sense of romance? Ain't you watching the show?" moaned Marty. Gil knew he would try to litigate his way out of a fast departure from the theater tonight. Marty would make a great lawyer—if he could just stay on the right side of the law long enough.

"The show on stage is just fine," Gil replied, pointing Marty into the last empty seat. "It was the one at intermission I object to." The residents of Homestretch Farm were going to set the world record for quick exits when this little production was over. And the subject of tomorrow's Bible study had just been changed to the topic of self-control.

Emily and Janet slipped into their seats just before the house lights went down. Emily caught Gil's eye and mouthed, "Okay?"

"Fine," he mouthed back, although nothing felt fine at all. Not a blessed thing.

Chapter Six

Stretching out on her couch after the show, Emily let Edith Piaf's sweet, sharp tones pour French drama into the air. The woman had the kind of voice that dripped with passion for life and love. So *French*.

Before Ash's death, Emily had been given to daydreams of Paris. She'd talk to Ash about yearning to stroll the Parisian streets, see the Eiffel Tower and eat pastry until she popped, but there had never been enough time or money to even consider it. They always told each other they'd go "when he established himself."

And then he was gone. Now, even if she could find the time and funds, Emily didn't think she could bear to go to Paris alone.

Lemonade and bake sales in the high-school gym was a far cry from café and croissants on the French Riviera. But maybe someday she would find herself on a velvet divan tucked into the corner of a small Parisian flat. A charming little abode with a wrought-iron balcony and polished wooden floors that only barely muffle the sound of the starving musician who lives downstairs and plays classical piano till all hours of the night.

Did she blame the bystander at Ash's murder for the loss of that dream? A large part of her did. She never could get over the ache that he—whoever he was—could have done *something* to stop it. Emily blamed the man who killed Ash, surely. But he had been caught and was paying for his crime. There was some closure in knowing justice had been served there. But there had been no justice yet for the mysterious witness the police said had been at the scene. He'd just watched, according to Ash's last words. To know your last moments on earth were spent watching someone ignore your pleas for help. How hideous.

They'd never been able to find him. Never been able to discover if it was someone who knew Ash or the murderer, or just some man who *could* have been at the right place at the right time but chose instead to do nothing.

She was still angry, four years later. She hadn't really healed. Maybe giving that speech would help her along. It could cause one person to act differently if they found themselves in that kind of situation. Ash would have liked that. It would help his death to mean something. But a public speech? It would take a lot of strength. But then again, she was already stronger than she ever thought she could be. She started West of Paris with some of the life insurance money and a business loan, and she'd made it this far. She'd even made her January loan payment. January, the hardest retail month of all. Two weeks ago, it had loomed over her as an impossible feat. A near-constant entry in her prayer journal. And, praise God, her prayer had been answered. Granted, it had been answered in a strange way—scruffy thugs suddenly paying attention to personal hygiene—but it had been answered. Emily sent up a quick prayer that the lesson the guys had learned tonight was that a clean, nicely dressed man turned a woman's head, not the scent of Lord Edmund's Pirate Soap.

And then there was Gil Sorrent. He almost never came into town—now he shows up with farmhands in tow at the community theatre musical? And why did she even care? He just happened to be in her field of vision, so that she could see him easily when she looked to stage right. She'd always liked that light-blue color, so it wasn't that his shirt was particularly noteworthy or anything.

As a matter of fact, Gil Sorrent was such a sourpuss, she'd been known to avoid him. She knew he was a man of faith, and she'd known plenty of lives turned around by God, but that still didn't stop her from thinking he seemed far too severe for such a ministry. If they had fun on the farm, it never showed. On the rare times he did show up in town, he was always herding them this way and that, always watching them like a hawk, making sure they toed the line.

You couldn't argue with the man's results, though. Every year Gil Sorrent managed a transformation that she'd have thought impossible. When she thought about it, Homestretch Farm was one of the strongest witnesses Emily knew to the power of Jesus Christ in a troubled life. Sandy put it best: "Men at Homestretch started out as hoodlums and ended up as heroes."

Othello began inching closer to the croissant she had on the coffee table. She waved the cat away. "Oh no you don't, mister. That pastry's all mine." Dissuaded, Othello began swatting at the brochure that sat at the other end of the table, the one on ATM-unit designs. Howard had dropped it off at the shop in the afternoon, reluctantly muttering something about "valuing her input." It sounded more like he'd tolerate her input under pressure, but Emily decided that worked just as well. Howard would still get his user fees, no matter what the dastardly little machines looked like, so he had little reason to grumble.

Unless you counted the mandatory contribution to the Beautification Fund. That, Emily guessed, stuck in his craw more than anything else. Well, good. It was high time someone forced Howard to be a little less mayoral and a little more philanthropic. If Howard Epson became another of Gil Sorrent's amazing transformations, she'd be fine with that. Maybe even Gil'd be fine with that.

What Emily was sure Gil wouldn't be fine with, however, was how many of his guys were bound to show up in West of Paris on Wednesday to buy more soap. Wednesday was their morning in town. Emily guessed that at the rate her nose told her they were using their current bars of soap, they'd be looking to restock if not to horde it. They'd garnered a fair amount of attention at the play—mostly just by showing up nicely dressed—but she doubted the guys saw it that way. Would more Pirate Soap make things better or worse? She had to find a way to keep her unlikely new customers and wise them up without giving Sorrent reason to stage a farm-wide boycott of her shop. But what?

"I need a new plan," she said as she snatched the last of the croissant out of Othello's hungry gaze.

Twenty minutes later, smack dab in the middle of Edith Piaf's soaring finale to "La Vie En Rose," it came to her.

Emily wasn't that surprised to see Gil Sorrent come in on the heels of his guys as the shop opened Wednesday morning. Even though it was often Ethan who supervised their in-town visits, Emily doubted the hands even sneezed without Gil's permission this morning. He probably picked out their pastries from the bakery personally.

When they shuffled into West of Paris, followed by a grumpy looking Sorrent, half of them were still licking icing off their fingers. She was ready. She had a stack of index cards in the left corner of the cash register, and a dozen new bars of Lord Edmund's Pirate soap under the counter. The fact that the bars had numbers matching the index cards, well, that'd come to light soon enough.

"Morning, ma'am," said the big one. "I reckon you know why we're here."

Over their heads, Gil Sorrent's expression broadcast "So now what are you going to do?" He wore a brown leather coat that looked as if it belonged to a man who worked hard, jeans and a faded green sweater over a T-shirt. Comfortable, but not unkempt. He dangled an enormous set of keys from one hand while he held a big cup of coffee in the other.

"Indeed I do," Emily replied. "But I'm afraid things have changed a bit from our last transaction."

The one with dark hair pointed a finger at the group. "I *told* you she'd up the price."

Sorrent started to say something, but Emily held up one hand and smiled. "The price stays a fair four dollars." She injected all the confidence she could muster into her voice, even though most of them seemed two feet taller than her. "But y'all still haven't wised up, so your next sales are gonna have a few strings attached. Line up, please."

Sorrent's eyes widened under the dark fringe of his hair. He stopped fidgeting with his key ring. The young men gaped at each other, then clumsily sorted themselves into a line. Emily pulled the first bar of soap from her box and held it up. All eyes followed. She pointed to the wrapper. "I'm guessing by now you noticed each of these bars includes a verse of scripture on the inside of the wrapper?"

Sorrent's face registered a curious sort of understanding, but the surprised faces of the hands told Emily they paid little attention to the wrapper in their rush to use the soap. "The verse that's inside is also coded right here on the label." She pointed to the number code the Edmundsons had shown her when she bought the soaps. She'd wondered why it was there, but now it seemed God had simply provided her with what she needed to pull this off. Emily caught Sorrent's glance as she continued, "I wrote down the verse for each of the soaps on these cards. I'll assign you each one bar of soap, and I'll keep the card with its matching verse. Come back next Wednesday showing me you've memorized the verse on the wrapper, and I'll sell you your bar."

Jaws dropped. Well, she'd fully expected that.

It was another brilliant plan, if she said so herself. The boys got their soap, she got her money, God got a foothold into their troubled young souls and the world had another week to get over its misguided fascination with Lord Edmund's Pirate Soap. It was an ideal compromise.

Gil took a long sip of coffee. "Ms. Montague," he said slowly, "that's a fine, fine thing." He turned to the men. "You were each going to get a memory verse in your Bible studies tomorrow, but it seems the Good Lord and Emily Montague just beat me to the punch. What do you know?"

The hands erupted out of their neat line to express frustration in a variety of loud ways.

"I need to change one thing, though," Sorrent said, pushing through the group to set his coffee down on the counter.

"You do?"

"I'd like to assign the verses. I know these troublemakers, and I know what they ought to be learnin'. Would you agree to my looking over your assignments and making a few adjustments if need be?"

Emily had to agree that his input—especially if it gained his approval—could only be an improvement on her plan for the guys. All scripture was useful, but applied scripture from a man who knew their strengths and weaknesses, well that would be a powerful thing, indeed. "I can't see why not."

Gil ignored the groans that echoed out behind him and extended a hand. "You've got yourself a deal, Ms. Montague," he said as he shook her hand. "I'll come back at eleven-thirty after I've dropped this motley crew off for their haircuts." He picked up his coffee and took a satisfied gulp.

The haircuts were evidently news, for the chorus of groans rose still higher in volume. Gil turned to face them. "What are you all grousin' about? You were the ones fussin' with your hair all last week."

"I don't want no buzz cut!" declared a tall youth with a head full of braided dark locks.

"Nobody said nothin' about no buzz cuts. You'll all get what you want, provided it's not spiked or purple. Now just give me a moment to square away things with Ms. Montague, will you?"

He turned back to Emily. "I'll come back without them in about an hour and we can match up guys with verses. Suit you?"

"Fine, Mr. Sorrent. I'd welcome your input."

"More than Howard welcomes yours?" He managed something close to a smile, and she noticed the corners of his dark-brown eyes crinkled up.

Emily laughed. "That wouldn't be hard, I'm afraid."

"Howard'll come round. And if he doesn't, he's still got to do it anyways, so it won't matter. See you at eleven-thirty."

Emily stared after Sorrent as he left the shop. Had he just attempted humor? Nearly smiled? Here she was, expecting a battle, and she just received not only cooperation but a small dose of encouragement. Amazing.

She shook her head and tucked the index cards away. Maybe there was more to Gil Sorrent than she first thought.

Chapter Seven

Twenty or so minutes later, a frazzled mother came into the shop with an infant boy and a toddler girl tucked into a double stroller. The infant was fast asleep. The girl had the red-eyed pout of someone who'd just finished crying long and hard. She glowered at Emily through wet lashes from over the top of a sippy cup held in bright red mittens. The woman didn't look too far from a crying jag of her own. Her hair was starting to pull out of its haphazard ponytail and something had spilled down the side of her sweatshirt. It had obviously been a rough morning for this little trio.

Emily reached into a basket below the counter and took out one of the little felt daisies she kept for just such occasions. She came around the counter and handed the toy flower to the toddler, who gave a shuddering sigh and pulled off her mittens to inspect it, dropping them distractedly to the ground. The mother gave an exhausted groan, as if she'd spent the entire morning picking up discarded mittens.

Emily bent over and fetched the mittens for her. "Take a deep breath and enjoy the quiet," she said, handing her the mittens. "Then you can tell me how I can help you."

The woman did as she was told, and for a moment she teetered on the edge of the crying spell hiding just behind her eyes. Then she took a second deep breath, and it pulled her back a bit from the verge of tears. *Lavender does that,* Emily thought, glad she had used that particular oil to scent the shop today. *Calms the spirit.*

"I'm looking for the Peace Soap." The mother shook out her shoulders to stand a little taller.

"You must mean the Edmundson's Fruit of the Spirit soaps?"

"I guess." She brushed at a spot on her sleeve as the little girl started singing to herself.

"They come in a whole bunch of scents. Did you like the peace scent in particular?" Emily led the woman over toward the display.

"I don't know what it smells like, but if it smells like peace, I want it. I'm sure I can't remember what peace smells like. I'm not sure I can remember what clean smells like."

Emily picked up the sample Peace Soap and handed it to the woman. "You might find several scents that appeal to you."

The mother held it to her nose and inhaled. Twice. "Oh, that's nice. Yes, I like that one. I'll take three."

"I'm partial to the Joy Soap myself." Emily selected two additional peace bars, discreetly turning a few over to ensure the woman got three different verse labels. The Edmundsons had made sure that each type of soap came with five different verses. "Try this." She held out a bar.

"Ooo, that one smells good, too. But I'll stick with the Peace Soaps. I need all the peace I can get."

"They're a handful, aren't they?" Emily offered, nodding toward the children.

"Some days. You a mom?"

"I…um…missed my chance," Emily said awkwardly, "but every woman alive knows the power of a long hot bath with beautifully scented soaps."

"I'm lucky I get five minutes in the shower alone, so I'm ready to try anything. Hey, I'm calmer already and I haven't even paid for it yet."

"I like to think of my shop as a calming place." Emily began to ring up the woman's purchases. "You know, the Middleburg Community Church has a weekly mothers' group with free babysitting. I bet the company of other hardworking moms would do you a world of good. That comes to twelve seventy-two."

The woman handed over her credit card. When Emily handed her the bag, she dug through the tissue paper to pull out the soap and sniffed it again.

"Lavender is very calming," Emily explained as she wrote the phone number of the church and the name of the woman who ran the ministry on a card. She reached over and dropped the card in the bag. "Tell them Emily Montague sent you. Maybe we could do a spa night for the whole group, or just some of your friends."

"Maybe."

Emily pointed to the girl who had fallen asleep in the stroller with the felt daisy in her hand. The mom smiled and tucked a soft pink blanket around her. "See," said Emily, "it's better already. You'll be fine."

"Maybe," the woman repeated, sighing.

"Lavender will only get you so far. Come to our church and find some real peace, won't you?" The woman said she'd think about it, and headed out the door with lighter steps than when she'd walked in.

No sooner had the mother left than Gil Sorrent came back into the shop. He stood, finger pointing out the window. "I just…" He fumbled for the next words, wagging his pointing finger. "There was…I just saw a woman walking down the street sniffing your soap. She looked as if she was gonna inhale the thing."

"She was in here just now."

"That's…that's just weird. You know that, don't you?"

Emily bristled. So much for Gil Sorrent being friendly. "Nobody's going to die from enjoying the scent of a bar of soap, Mr. Sorrent. That woman has every right to spend her money how she chooses, and I actually may have gotten her interested in our church's moms' group during the sale, if you must know." Emily couldn't remember the last time someone got her dander up so fast.

"You can't have people going nuts over soap like that." He stuffed a hand in one pocket. "You can't tell me you're okay with that."

"Well, I admit some may find her reaction a bit extreme."

"Extreme?"

"But I make it a point not to judge my customers." Emily felt the desire to defend the poor woman well up inside her out of nowhere. "Parenting is hard work, and she'd had a rough morning from the looks of it. I've just made an inroad with her for our church. So what if it was over a bar of soap that she really likes? It's good soap, and it has a very peaceful smell."

Gil broadened his stance, his boots thumping against the wood floor. The man was tall and he knew how to use it. "You're defending the stuff," he balked. "We've spent half the weekend trying to get my guys to see reason and now you're defending the stuff?"

Emily crossed her arms. "I'm defending her right not to be made fun of by the likes of you."

"That woman looked as if she might take a bite if she went on much longer."

"Gil Sorrent, you're being ridiculous—"

The bell on the shop door jingled as an older man wandered in, silencing their argument. "May I help you?"

"Please. There's a sour old lady living next to me who used to smile all the time." The man leaned heavily on a dark wood cane. "I'm looking for that kindness soap they said you sell." He adjusted his bolo tie and winked at Emily. "It's her birthday tomorrow, and I sure would take to seeing some kindness from her again."

Gil's scowl radiated from his pores as he pretended to be inspecting some hand towels.

Emily smiled at the old man and steered him in the direction of a display of lace handkerchiefs. "Ladies of a certain age," she said as if revealing a secret, "have a fondness for scented hankies, you know." She gently touched his elbow.

"Hankies—that's a good idea, too. I reckon she would like something like that." He picked up the Edmundson's Kindness Soap. "So what does kindness smell like?"

Emily heard Gil stifle a derisive snort from behind her. "It's a vanilla sort of smell," she said, "with a hint of butter and cinnamon. Like something baking, I think."

A twinkle played in the old man's watery eyes. "That'll do nicely." He took the bar she held out for him and sniffed it. "What do you know? It *does* smell kind."

"There's a Bible verse inside each wrapper about the value of kindness," Emily offered, pitching her voice up a bit to make sure Gil heard her. "That'll help more than the soap."

"The Good Book's always a help, little lady. You'll wrap both those up all pretty for me, won't you?"

Gil could barely believe she'd just sold another bar of the stuff. "See what I mean?" Gil barked the minute the old man left.

"So I'm not supposed to sell him what he came in for, just because it might be a bit misguided? Do you know how many truly misguided gifts are given in this world?"

"Well, at least we agree on the misguided part," he replied. Hadn't they just talked about how to redirect his guys from their foolish purchases? Now she was defending frazzled mothers inhaling the soaps and old men squandering their fixed incomes on them? No, this had to stop now. "You know what? I've changed my mind. I don't think there's any need for us to agree on verse assignments. My guys aren't going to spend one more dime on your soaps."

Gil was sure she was going to haul off at him after he said that. She was probably counting on a nice bundle of sales from those boys. He waited for her to lay into him. He wanted her to see how little effect her ranting and raving would have.

She did neither. He'd essentially just announced a Homestretch Farm boycott of her store, but she just stared at him, as if examining him under a microscope. Was that supposed to be threatening? Could anyone even begin to look threatening in a sweater that color?

She came around the counter and crossed one fuzzy yellow arm over the other. "You don't spend much time with your niece, do you?"

Gil didn't see what that had to do with anything. "Huh?"

"How many teens have you had up at your stables? And you still don't know that the fastest way to get anyone under twenty-five to do something is to forbid him to do it?"

Well, of course he knew that. But this was different. He wasn't sure how, but it was. "I can handle my guys."

"Oh, I'm sure you can. There's no one in Middleburg who would argue that Gil Sorrent can't get the job done." The way she said it wasn't entirely complimentary. "You and I can go a round on the ethics of forbidding your farm-hands to buy these bars, but I'll tell you one thing: if you outlaw these soaps, I'm one hundred percent certain those guys will find a way in here." She fished out the stack of index cards she'd brandished earlier and clicked the top of her pen. "Wouldn't you rather have them coming in on terms we set than sneaking in behind your back?"

He stared at her. She had him. He knew it, she knew it. "I ain't got time to do this now."

"Then I'll just come by the farm this afternoon. I have to go out that way anyway."

If he were half as smart as he ought to be, he'd just walk out and put this fiasco behind him. The whole thing seemed wrong anyhow. He didn't see how adding Bible verses to the mix—or having Emily up to the farm—was gonna solve anything. Then again, he'd had no luck getting the guys to memorize verses in the past. Could he ignore the possibility that the ultimate motivation was right in front of him? If he went along with her plan, the guys would find out soon enough that soap isn't the way to a woman's heart. They actually *had* been cleaner this week than any time in recent memory. The smell, while not his favorite by a long shot, wasn't that much worse than anything else a nose could come across in a stable.

When you ask God for a match, don't go griping when he hands you a gallon of gasoline.

He tossed his business card down on the table. "One-thirty?"

She picked up the business card and headed back around the counter. "Fine by me. And thanks."

"For…?"

"For Howard." She tucked his card into a little old-fashioned looking handbag she pulled from a drawer. After a pause she added, "And this."

Gil stared at the handbag and wondered if this woman owned any shoes that had any business being hear a horse barn. "I still think I'll regret it."

Chapter Eight

Emily was just getting ready to leave when Dinah Hopkins poked her head in the store. "Whatcha got in the sneaky thank-you department?" Dinah's bakery down the street had probably been overrun with farmhands this morning. Emily didn't mention that the sugar rush had come straight to her store after visiting Dinah's—it seemed too complicated an issue to get into just then, although she was sure Dinah would have backed her up on her creative sales scheme.

Emily and Dinah had become friends in the months since Dinah moved to town and took over the bakery. Emily liked Dinah's enthusiasm for life. She was a lot like a young Sandy Burnside—the same kick but far less nail polish.

As she always did whenever she saw Dinah, Emily began humming "Someone's in the kitchen with Dinah" from the old song almost no one remembered anymore.

"You know, Emily," Dinah said as she pulled off her gloves and began fingering through a stack of vintage tea towels on the shelf by the windows, "there wasn't ever a time when that was funny. Ever." Dinah still had flour smudges on her pants and she wore flip-flops even though it was almost February.

"Thank-yous aren't supposed to be sneaky." Emily walked over to her. "They should be heartfelt and gracious. If thank-you is worth saying, it's worth saying face-to-face. What's up?"

"Peter Epson was in the bakery yesterday." Peter, a slightly geeky young man just a few years out of high school, was Howard Epson's son. For as large a character as Howard the Mayor was, Peter stumbled along in his father's shadow. He was a nice kid, polite and all, but somehow he'd never lived up to the high-achiever expectations his father had for him. Peter was, mostly, average. A nice average, perhaps a meek average, but not anyone who'd ever show up in the "most likely to" column of the yearbook. His one and only achievement was that he was a reporter for the local paper.

"Doing an exposé on the fat content of your fudge brownies," Emily teased, "or just taste-testing?"

"Ha-ha." Dinah pointed at her with a Victorian hat pin she'd just pulled from one of Emily's displays. "You're in a fine humor today, Ms. Montague. No, he was just in looking at some very Valentiney cake designs." Dinah raised a red eyebrow. Dinah had the brightest red hair Emily had ever seen and insisted it was her natural color, although Emily had her doubts. "I think our cub reporter's got a crush. Be on the lookout, he might end up in here. He took forever deciding, then decided *not* to get a cake. But that's not really why I'm here."

"You're here looking for sneaky thank-yous."

"You got it." She pulled Emily over to the counter by the

elbow, whispering in the voice of someone revealing a juicy secret. "While Peter was in, I heard him talking to a buddy of his about being at the library. He said he freaked out when he stumbled upon Audrey Lupine crying way back in the periodicals section. She was talking quietly to someone about leaving the library. Said she didn't feel appreciated. That no one cared much about librarians anymore."

"Audrey? How could she be feeling down when she's just done such a fabulous job in the musical?"

"Well, I think that's just it—all that attention in the musical made her feel invisible at work. I think she needs a pick-me-up. A little goody from the Library Board to let her know we appreciate her years of service. She'll have been there ten years tomorrow." Dinah was about the least likely Vice Chairperson of the Middleburg Library Board Emily could ever imagine, but she'd done an outstanding job of balancing out Howard, who was, of course, Chairman of the Library Board and nearly everything else.

Emily grinned. "Aren't you *in* the goody business?"

"That's just it. If I whip something up for her, everyone'll know it was me. I want this to be dramatic. Sort of a 'secret admirer.' But heartfelt. Come on, you gotta have something in here that'll do the trick."

Emily drummed her fingers against the counter, inventorying the possibilities. This sounded like a job for Edmundson's Faithfulness Soap and a few of those exquisite petit-point bookmarks she'd picked up last month. "I've got to run out on an errand later this afternoon. I'll pack up something—free of charge as my bit toward the cause—and leave it all wrapped at the bakery in about twenty minutes. That way even you won't know what it is, and it'll all be a grand surprise."

Dinah grinned. "I knew you'd think of something. Sign the card from the Library Board. I've got a meeting over there tonight so I can slip it in without anyone noticing. It'll be sitting pretty on her desk when she comes in tomorrow morning."

As she pulled her car onto Old Frankfort Pike that afternoon, Emily found herself rethinking the wisdom of her offer to visit Homestretch. Had she suddenly forgotten she didn't like horses? That she was actually afraid of horses?

This was a distinct disadvantage in a place like Middleburg, where most of the town owed its livelihood—directly or indirectly—to equestrian pursuits. Despite living in "the horse capital of the world" for so many years, Emily had never managed to transform herself into a "horse person."

Homestretch Farm sat nestled between two rolling hillsides just north of the Pike. It was a modest farm by bluegrass standards, where equine housing could run well beyond nice and into luxurious and even opulent. Many farms had stables nicer than most homes, and twice as large. Homestretch was mid-size, about 250 acres by Emily's guess, with a friendly dotting of green-and-white buildings across the compound. Given Gil's usual state of dress, she wasn't sure if she would find a rough-and-tumble farm, or if his tight-ship mentality would mean he ran a neat operation.

Pulling up to the iron gate that led onto Homestretch, Emily could see that Gil ran an efficient farm. Two curving stone walls with green-and-white light fixtures held an electric iron gate. At the center of the gate was a green square with a white galloping horse—she recognized that as the Homestretch Farm logo. She'd noticed it on some of the guys' T-shirts when they'd come into the shop, and a smaller version of it hung from Gil's keychain. She hit the intercom button, announced herself, and watched the gates swing open. "You don't have to go near the horses," she told herself as she steered her powder-blue VW down the lane. "Just because he told you to meet him in the largest barn doesn't mean you'll be near horses. She drove past the enormous rustic white main house with its green trim and gray slate roof, past the dorm-type building she guessed to be where the hands lived, and still farther back to where the offices and barns were. There were five barns in all, but as Gil had said, it was obvious which was the main barn.

A black horse looked up as she drove by, its gaze following her as she drove past. The animal's dark round eyes stared over the white fence as if to say "Are you sure that's a *real* car?" Emily reckoned you could fit her entire VW bug in the bed of Gil's big red truck and still have room to spare.

A second horse thudded by on her right, trotting fast, carrying a bony young man who seemed eight sizes too small for his T-shirt. He had thick black dreadlocks hanging out from under a baseball cap he wore backward. She recognized him from earlier that morning as the one who didn't want a haircut. He wore a gold chain so large she wondered how it didn't knock in his teeth as he bumped up and down on the horse. In her rearview mirror, Emily watched him twist around to watch her car go by.

She recognized Gil's towering outline standing in the barn's open double doors facing out into the pastures. It was like staring at the cover of a horse-farmer textbook: big man in blue jeans, work coat, boots and heavy gloves. He was even holding a rope in one hand while he rested his other elbow on some rake-like farming implement. Leaning casually against the door frame, Gil was shouting directions to another young man who was leading a small horse around a ring on what looked like an oversize leather leash.

The noise of her car caught his attention, and he began to put down the equipment and walk toward her as she parked on the patch of asphalt that stretched out in front of the barn.

It looked to be a well-kept barn, as tidy as Emily imagined barns could get. It was an unusual L-shape, with a round room joining the two wings of stables. That was distinctive enough, but as she got out of the car, Emily noticed what looked to be perhaps a dozen cats sitting on the roof of the barn.

Gil Sorrent didn't strike her as a cat person.

A second look revealed that the cats weren't real. The man had china cats—and a few other creatures, from the look of things—mounted on the roof of his barn. Gil Sorrent definitely did not look like the type of man to collect curios, either. Shielding her eyes against the sun, she pointed up with the other hand toward the faux felines. "Couldn't afford the real thing?" she asked.

"Real cats would probably be cheaper," he said, a grin sneaking across his face. "And we have a few of those, somewhere. But these are a French tradition. Left over from the previous owner, mostly. Someone told me they're worth a lot of money, but I didn't believe him."

"Why not?"

"Cuz when I told him to climb up there and take the critters home himself, he declined."

"Maybe he was just afraid of heights?"

"Maybe, but he didn't look much afraid of money, so I figure if they weren't incentive enough for him, I'd just let 'em be. They tend to surprise people, and the guys spend hours giving them goofy names each year, so they make for an entertainment of sorts." French ceramics on the roof for entertainment? What next?

Gil shouted a brief direction to the young man behind him and hung the rake on a wall peg. "And they never fail to start a conversation." He walked over to a small fridge tucked under a table and opened it. He plucked out two green bottles of Ale-8 and held one out to her.

"No thanks, can't stand that stuff," she said, pushing a hand out at him.

"What? You don't drink Kentucky's official soft drink? I thought everybody here loved this stuff." He angled the bottleneck on the edge of the table and whacked off the cap with a practiced move. "Want something else?"

Emily was trying to calculate the distance between the small horse and her—it seemed safe enough. "I'm not really thirsty. And I didn't start out a local, so maybe they'll forgive me one day for not taking a liking to Ale-8." *And not taking a liking to horses, either,* Emily added in the back of her mind.

He caught her expression. "You don't ride?"

Ah, now here was a quandary. When, exactly, is the best time to admit to a horse farmer that you're afraid of horses? Especially a born reformer like Gil Sorrent, who might just haul you up on a horse to prove to you that you just haven't met the *right* horse?

"Not much." *More like not at all. Do carousel ponies count?*

At this moment, the equine in question decided to give

a very nasty display of temperament and knock over the young man leading him around, sending him to the ground dangerously near a pile of...how to put it delicately...essence of horse. He muttered a string of what was surely impolite Spanish at the horse.

Gil chuckled. "I've told you before, Paulo, you take your eye off that horse and she's gonna show you why it's a bad idea. Your brain can't leave the barn every time a lady walks in, *amigo*. Next time we might be mending your bones instead of just washing your jeans." He turned to Emily. "Now Lady Macbeth here," he said, pointing to an enormous horse Emily had not even noticed because it was standing so still off to one side of the barn, "she knows how to behave. She's the horse for someone like you."

An *enormous* horse. How had she not seen the huge, possibly dangerous horse right in front of her? Emily took a step backward. "I'm thinking there just really isn't a horse for me. Riding's not my thing."

"That's what I said," Paulo offered, dusting himself off as he returned from tying up the feisty little horse that had knocked him down, "until I met The Lady. She's the horse for everyone. 'Specially people who say they don't like horses."

"I never said I didn't like horses," Emily countered.

"Back up any more and you'll be clear out of the barn," Gil snorted. "That screams 'I don't like horses' to me."

"I tell you, Ms. Montague, there's nothing to be afraid of. *Nada.* Not with Lady Macbeth."

"Have you read *Macbeth,* Paulo? Lady Macbeth is not a nice lady. If I aim to get on a horse anytime in the future, it's certainly not going to be one named after a murderess." Lady Macbeth stomped as if she found that insulting, which made Emily wonder if the horse understood English.

"Well, I'm sure *she* hasn't read *Macbeth*." Gil replied, now checking the large horse's tack as though he was going to hoist her up there any second. "She's the gentlest horse here. I had a four-year-old up on her the other day."

"She was more scared than you," Paulo said, evidently under the misconception that such a remark would help.

"She's huge," Emily gulped.

"Her size makes her easier to stay up on. Just think of her as a walking couch." He polished off his Ale-8 and eyed Emily. "You know, I think now's as good a time as any to get over it. Right here, right now, before you have a chance to talk yourself out of it. I'll make it easy for you. Stand up on that wall over there and I'll sidle her up right beside you so you can just slide on. I'll be holding the reins all the time. Five minutes. I won't put her above a walk, I promise."

Emily stared at him, then stared at Paulo, calculating her chances of death and dismemberment. The horse seemed eleven feet tall.

"Five minutes on the back of one nice horse," Gil cajoled. "It'll do you wonders." Lady Macbeth gave a soft whinny of encouragement.

"My *abuela* could do five minutes on 'Beth," Paulo remarked brightly.

"Paulo's daring grandmother aside, you can do this," Gil said, taking her basket of files and her handbag from her and laying them on a table behind him. "Tell you what. I'll buy three bars of the smelliest soap you got if you do this."

She'd seem like the lowliest of cowards if she couldn't agree to this. But this horse was enormous. Still, it'd be hard to find a better way to get on Sorrent's good side.

Slowly, without taking her eyes off the horse, Emily walked over to the little stone wall steps. She clutched the railing and walked up the half dozen steps until she was level with the horse's back. Gil gave the reins to Paulo and moved over to help Emily. "Just put your left foot out over here." She complied, thinking how odd it felt to be looking down on a man as large as Gil Sorrent. He helped her slide easily—if gingerly—onto the saddle. The horse obliged by standing perfectly still while Emily found her balance. She could feel the warmth of the horse through the material of her pant legs, the powerful and dangerous muscles flexing, her massive ribs expanding as she breathed. It was definitely not like sitting on any couch she'd ever known.

"Take a few deep breaths up there," Gil said, his voice a warm and encouraging tone. He waited until she looked at him. "Good. Ready to move?"

"Okay," she said shakily.

Gil took the reins back from Paulo. "We're gonna walk out along that path there," he said, using that same even voice, "Nice and slow." With a soft click of his tongue and the slightest tug on the reins, he led Lady Macbeth and Emily slowly out into the pasture.

Chapter Nine

"You know, that wasn't so bad," Emily said as she followed Gil to the offices after her five-minute foray into equine relations. "I'm not in any hurry to do it again, though."

"You done good. Course, I can't have you breaking my perfect teaching record, neither. I appreciate your success. And you can bill me for the stinkiest soaps you got—a deal's a deal." Gil opened the door and flipped a bank of switches to illuminate a surprisingly sleek office with every high-tech gadget imaginable. She counted at least three computer monitors, two printers, a bunch of walkie-talkie-looking things, and a wireless headset. Not to mention a stack of spreadsheet printouts that covered his desk and the PDA and cell phone he pulled out of his jean pockets before he sat down. Emily half expected to find little horse icons wandering around on a radar screen somewhere.

"It looks like an electronics store in here," she said, scanning the myriad of technology. "You run a high-tech operation."

"I like to make use of improvements. There's still no

substitute for a good head on your shoulders, but there's a heap of helpful technology out there these days." One side of his mouth turned up. "Besides, it impresses the guys and makes me look cool. I can use every advantage I can get with that lot." Emily was amazed at how a man could look rugged and slick—it didn't seem as if those two adjectives could apply to the same man at once.

"So why can't you think of the soap as an advantage?" Emily ventured.

She didn't give up, did she? Gil put a boot on his desk. She looked so funny, sitting there clutching that basket and little handbag of hers. She carried her town council papers in a straw basket, too. Other people used tote bags or briefcases, but Emily Montague seemed to have a basket for everything. It was like doing business with Little Red Riding Hood.

She sat with her feet tucked tightly underneath her, as if she were afraid the farm would seep in under the door to steal her away and stuff her into a pair of overalls. How did someone living in Kentucky look so lost on a horse farm? And why did it amuse him so that she did? But it wasn't a make-fun-of-you kind of amusement, it was something else, something more like a you'll-come-round kind of affection. It was as if he somehow knew she'd cope with it even if she didn't know.

"I said I'd give your soap-for-verses plan a try, didn't I?" he said, addressing her question.

She reached into her basket. "Have you got a list of your men handy? That'd be a good place to start. I brought my Bible and the list of verses."

"Miles ahead of you." He pointed to the SMART board on the wall behind her. "Watch this."

She spun her chair around as Gil punched a sequence of keys on his computer. *Oh, why not pull out all the stops?* He hit a few more to turn on the voice-activated commands. The SMART board, an oversize interactive gizmo that was part computer monitor, part chalkboard, lit up. With a few keystrokes, Gil cleared a task schedule he'd been working on this morning and pulled up a blank page. She looked over her shoulder at him, clearly understanding he was showing off and—what do you know?—enjoying it. He grabbed the headset off his desk, slipped it on and said into the microphone, "Open file. Hand list."

Emily let out a small sound of amazement as an alphabetized list of names appeared on the screen.

"Table. Column. Tile," Gil said, and the list became the first column of a chart and shrank to the bottom of the screen. "Open Bible." An electronic Bible program appeared on the top of the screen, so that the screen held both sets of information. "Which translation do we need?" he said, covering the microphone with one hand.

"How many do you have in there?"

"All of them. Including Greek and Latin, if you're feeling like serving up a mean challenge to my guys."

She smiled. "New International will do just fine."

Gil told the program to load, and a tiny version of the Homestretch Farm logo appeared, and began spinning slowly. "Steve's little addition to my software," he said off the microphone. "The guy's gonna change the world if he doesn't blow it up first."

"No wonder so many of your guys have iPods—this is the first ever techno-farm." Emily watched as the SMART board whirred through its paces. Gil had to admit, it was his favorite purchase of the year.

"The government grants cover lots of their basic living expenses, but I give 'em each an iPod when they get here. For many of them, it's the first time they've had something expensive that they didn't steal or get stolen from them. Of course, I have ulterior motives. Since I bought 'em, I load 'em. They earn money in their iTunes accounts from me, and I screen their purchases. And, I get to pick one tune out of ten. You'd be amazed at the cool Christian music out there if you look around. Even Paulo doesn't wince anymore when he stumbles onto what I've loaded on there for him."

Emily turned and looked at him. He hadn't intended to go into a speech about his techno-savvy or how he wielded it to God's advantage. There was just something about that soft, sweet nature of hers that made him show off.

"That's incredibly creative," she said, with a sort of wonder in her voice that did things to the pit of his stomach. "And really effective, I bet. I wonder if anyone in Middleburg really knows all you do for these guys. Most people just think you work them so hard they don't have any energy left over to get into trouble."

"Well, that, too. But that'll only get you so far. My prayer is that I finally get through to the inside, not just tucker out the outside." Once again, he'd said far more than he planned. "Okay, let's start with the first verse you've got."

"Psalm 32:23."

Gil punched in the citation, and the words *The Lord protects the loyal but fully repays the arrogant* came up on the screen. "Good one. Could probably apply to all of them, but I'd have to say it's particularly useful to Larry." With a few keystrokes, Gil copied the verse and citation, and inserted it into the table next to Larry's name.

"Impressive."

Gil found himself hiding a smile. If he had to make a guess, he was betting she could barely set up the voicemail on her cell phone. Maybe he'd download a few gizmos for her as a favor. Make "Frére Jacques" her ringtone or something. "It has its uses. What's next?"

Emily shook her head as she drove through the Homestretch Farm gates. Gil seemed a complete turnaround from the man she'd considered him before. His program up there was far more comprehensive than she'd imagined. He worked with half a dozen government agencies to see that those young men got what they needed. They got GED courses, counseling, even literacy training if they couldn't read. He'd struck her as cold before she got a glimpse of his passion for giving the guys a second start in life. How much of his own money was he pouring into that farm? By the time they'd finished assigning verses to each hand, and Gil had talked about who they were and what kind of things each of them had faced in their young lives, Emily could see his commitment. He'd go to any lengths to turn those young men around. Do whatever it took.

She liked that about him.

She liked him.

Emily found she couldn't hold onto her old view of Gil Sorrent. She wasn't sure what to do with that just yet. As they'd worked through verse assignments, they'd talked about how each hand would take to the verse they'd chosen. She caught an energy in his eyes, as he paced the room, considering options and shifting verses around on that electric chalkboard thingy. Had she really gasped when he'd hit a key and two copies of what they'd written were printed out? That must have looked idiotic. He probably knew by now that she could barely work the speed dial on her telephone. She could only imagine he must think her a technophobic, horse-fearing sissy.

"I'm not!" she declared to the bobble-head Chihuahua on her dashboard. "I just prefer the peace and elegance of old-fashioned things. I like charming over cool, that's all. And it's perfectly sane to not need to spend every waking moment on top of a horse. Or address a felt dog while driving down the Old Frankfort Pike."

Chapter Ten

Gil was having lunch at Deacon's Grill with Mac, trying to get their proposal ready for the town council meeting that night, when Audrey Lupine burst into the Grill holding a bar of Faithfulness Soap. He was surprised librarians could be so loud. "How did you know?" she kept saying to Sandy Burnside, whose coffee break had been hijacked by the wildly emotional outburst. "However did you know?"

"Know what, honey?" Sandy said, foraging in her handbag for a tissue as Audrey was on the verge of tears.

"I was thinking of…of resigning at the end of the month. I've just felt so…useless. Everybody looks up whatever they need on the Internet now."

"You're a lot more than a reference librarian, Audrey, we depend on you in lots of ways," Sandy said, peering over Audrey's shoulder to the other Grill customers. With a raised eyebrow and a sharp glance, she cued them to echo her thoughts.

"Yeah, sure," "We need you" and "You're great"

bubbled up through the tiny crowd, making Audrey sniff and straighten herself.

"This morning, I found this bar of Edmundson's Faithfulness Soap on my desk—you know, that new stuff Emily sells down at her shop. It came with a note from the Library Board thanking me for my years of faithful service. I hadn't even realized it was my tenth anniversary there." Her voice dissolved into a wobbly sob on the last word.

"You *have* been faithful," Sandy said, handing her another tissue. "We know you have. And nobody needs a bar of soap to recognize that."

"What is it with the soap craze?" Mac whispered to Gil.

"You think I know?" Gil shot back. "How should I know?"

"Well, of course we know you deserve it," Howard Epson said importantly as he eased himself up out of a corner booth. Howard must not have been the one to give the gift, or he'd have taken credit by now. As a matter of fact, he looked a little put out that someone had done something notable *without* his input. "Who signed the card, anyway? You should thank 'em right away."

Audrey sniffled loudly as she rummaged through the lavender-colored tissue paper. Emily had her hand in there somewhere, or she knew who did, that much was sure. "Don't know." She pulled out the card. "It just says 'from the Library Board.'" Which seemed to miff Howard, for now someone had done something in the name of the Library Board without the permission of its esteemed chairman.

"I bet it's Dinah Hopkins. She's always doin' stuff like that," offered Sandy.

"But wouldn't Dinah just have sent something over from the bakery?" Audrey asked, blowing her nose. It made sense; Dinah owned the bakery and she was the generous type. "She knows I love her sticky buns."

"It doesn't really matter who got it for you," Sandy said. "It matters that you got it. That you know we think you've served us faithfully and we ain't in any hurry to loose you. You got that, darlin'?" With one arm she hugged Audrey's shoulders, while she cued applause from the Grill with the other behind Audrey's back.

It was all Gil could do not to shake his head in wonder as he stood there, applauding the town librarian and her faithfulness. The moment lunch was over, he took a little trip over to West of Paris. "All right, fess up," he said as he opened the door. "You gave the bar of Faithfulness Soap to Audrey, didn't you?"

"Pardon?"

She was acting casual, but she had a grin behind her eyes, he could see it.

"Dinah Hopkins bought it?" he asked.

"No, why?"

"Sandy?"

"No, *why?*"

"So you have no idea how somebody knew Audrey was thinking about quitting the library? No concept of how a bar of Faithfulness Soap mysteriously appeared on her desk to thank her for being so…you know…faithful?"

The grin came out from behind her eyes and played full across her face. "I may know something about that."

"But you're not telling." Gil stared at her. "Do you know everything about everyone around here?"

She didn't answer. She just stood there, grinning in that peach-colored lacy sweater of hers, without saying a word.

* * *

"There's got to be another solution. Widening that road is just plain wrong. Might as well just extend the freeway and put in an exit ramp with four fast food chains." Sandy Burnside took off her sparkly reading glasses and tossed them on the table.

Gil's composure hung by a thin thread, and Mac's wasn't far behind. It was already 10:00 p.m. and the council had three more items on the docket. If Howard hadn't gone off on one of his tangents and forced the whole council to listen to a detailed account of his last mare sale, they could have been a whole hour ahead.

"That's just the point, Ms. Burnside," said Mac. Gil recognized the I'm-trying-not-to-get-angry tone in Mac's voice. The two of them had worked for weeks on this recommendation, and most of the council members had dismissed it in a matter of seconds. "If we adjust the roadways to handle the traffic now, we won't have to do anything drastic in the future."

"I don't see why we have to do anything *now,*" Emily said, running her fingers down the tables of projections Mac's company had put in their proposal. "This report says we won't need that kind of infrastructure for another four years."

"But we've already agreed the road needs resurfacing *now,*" Gil countered. "If we do the expansion now, we'll save money in the long run."

"Save money," Sandy looked up, "or just make it easier to run those fancy computer cables?"

What have these people got against technology? Gil screamed in his head. "You've already seen what it's been like to try and retrofit the high school with Internet access.

People want Internet access. Tourists want Internet access. We need to plan ahead or we'll be forever playing catch-up."

"Well, I like *catsup*," Howard joked. Howard always thought any argument could be solved by the right joke. "Especially on hot dogs." Gil felt validated when everyone moaned. Not that it helped. He mentally counted to ten and tried to remember that two hours ago, he'd actually liked most of these people.

"I'm not asking you to say yes or no tonight," Gil said with the most level voice he could. "Let's all try to remember the principle of first reading and not squash an idea without really considering it."

"We've been considering it," Sandy Burnside sighed. "I don't think another two weeks is gonna make this idea seem any better to me."

"Well," Emily said, "I suppose we could look at these traffic projections again. I'm not convinced we know what kind of traffic we'll have in four years. I'd hate to add another lane only to find out we don't need it."

"But we *will* need it," Gil retorted. "We're already starting to need it. It's a four-lane road, people, not a shopping mall."

"One tends to lead to the other," Sandy said, bringing a chorus of agreement from around the table.

Gil looked straight at Emily. "Can we just let this sit for a session or two? Let people get used to the concept?" He hadn't expected anyone to say yes tonight. As a matter of fact, he'd fully anticipated that the project would only get approved with a two-year delay. To get anything done in Middleburg, you had to plan for resistance and compromise if not outright opposition. *Come on, Emily Montague, work with me here. I got a dozen guys memorizing scrip-*

ture in the shower—that says you know your way to a solution. He stared at her. He raised an eyebrow.

"A second reading is always a wise idea," she said. "If it still looks bad two weeks from now, we'll know our first impulses were right."

Gil exhaled.

"Fine, fine, I motion we table it for a second reading. Can we please move on now? We still have the report from the Character Day subcommittee," Sandy said.

"That would be you, Sandy," Howard joked. "You're a subcommittee of one."

"If anyone could be a subcommittee all by herself, it'd be Sandy," another member of the council said. Howard seemed annoyed that someone tagged on to his joke.

Sandy plunked her elbows down on the table. "Are y'all gonna let me say my piece or what? Some of us need a full eight hours of sleep, you know."

"Go ahead, Sandy, you've got the floor."

"I put a lot of thought into the Character Day speaker this year. This year's theme of integrity is highly important."

Emily felt the pit of her stomach drop down. Suddenly she was sure she'd made the wrong decision. Sandy would say her name and then the entire town council would groan their disapproval. She'd prayed over this for days, and she was sure—up until now—that this was something she should do. Now she was certain she'd misunderstood God and was about to make a fool of herself.

"So I'm pleased to announce that our own Emily Montague has accepted my request to be our Character Day speaker."

Emily thought the moment would feel bigger. Like

some kind of crucial watershed where her heart skipped and people's jaws dropped in shock. But it wasn't like that at all. Everyone looked at her, but there was no astonishment, no alarm. "Why, of course," said Audrey Lupine almost instantly. "Oh, hon, I can't think of anyone better."

"I know this is a big step for Emily, and I think we can all show her that we're in full-support of her decision to share her story with our young men and women." Sandy began to applaud enthusiastically, and the rest of the town council applauded, as well. Emily smiled, trying to look as if she was excited about this. It felt more like her stomach was full of tightly wound springs ready to uncoil at any moment. She was grateful when the meeting broke up ten minutes later.

Chapter Eleven

Gil hung back, waiting for Sandy and Emily to say goodnight to each other. He was impressed that Emily had taken what looked like a big step for her. *That woman has her fair share of courage,* he thought to himself as he caught up with her in the parking lot. "Congratulations. And hey, I owe you one—I thought we were dead in the water back there." His pickup looked enormous next to Emily's VW—an original Beetle, he noticed now, not the newer one introduced a few years ago.

"Thanks," she said, pulling on the fuzzy white beret she always wore. "And you don't owe me anything. I was only reminding the council of our usual practice of first reading. Robert's Rules of Order, I think—or it ought to be. I didn't do you any favors, just did my job."

"Well, I still feel like I owe you one. And like I said about the soap dishes, I always pay my debts. So how about a slice of Deacon's pie?" Deacon's Grill was the only place in Middleburg open at this time of night, but that didn't stop it from also being the maker of the best pie in the county.

It was Late-Night Movie Night back at the ranch anyhow, and he often stole away to Deacon's Grill to ensure he didn't have to sit through the guys' idea of fine cinema.

She opened her car door. He noticed her keychain was an antique silver spoon twisted into a swirly shape. "It's late."

"I happen to know Gina Deacon starts her baking at 10:00 p.m. If we time it right, we could get pie fresh out of the oven." If asked, he'd never let on that a shot at Deacon's just-baked pies was actually the driving force behind the creation of Late-Night Movie Night (and why Ethan was put in charge of the weekly event).

She paused for a moment, rolling down—*rolling down*—the too-old-to-be-electric window as her car sputtered to a start. It didn't sound like a very dependable car. "I'll meet you there," she said, pumping the gas pedal a few times. "First one in the door orders the coffee."

After he ordered blueberry and she ordered apple—à la mode, no less—Gil sat back in his seat. "I got a mess of printouts pinned up on my bunkhouse wall and boys quizzing each other on Bible verses, so yes, I owe you."

"Are you admitting I was right?"

"Maybe," he conceded. "Once we add more soap to the mix I might not keep my sense of gratitude."

They fell into an awkward silence. Bringing her to the Grill had seemed like such a good idea when he'd thought of it during the meeting—a friendly gesture. Only he wasn't really good at friendly gestures, and now it just felt uncomfortable. He looked out the window. It was starting to snow.

"I've always liked snow," she said. "It makes everything look clean."

"You run a bath shop. I think you've just got a thing for clean."

"I suppose you're right. I also like rain, and if you take away the mud, that's all about clean, too."

"I like mud. I got a dog named Mud, you know. Very fond of mud as a boy. Made my mama nuts." Now, where had that come from? What could have possessed Gil to suddenly bring up the subject of his childhood?

Emily eyed him. "I can just bet you gave your mama fits. You don't strike me as the minding kind. What does Gil stand for, anyway? Gilbert? Gilligan? I gotta admit, none of those fit you at all."

Now that was just a little too much personal revelation. "That information is dispensed on a need-to-know basis and I don't think you need to know."

She got that analytical look on her face again, and he could just bet she was pondering possible "Gil" names. He stared right back, as if challenging her not to press the issue. "I suppose I don't," she relented.

He chose a diversionary topic. "So how did West of Paris get its name? What's with all the French?"

Her face took on a bittersweet smile. "It's a bit of a story, actually. I've always had a sort of fascination with Paris. Took French in high school, watched every movie set in Paris ever made, that sort of thing. It just seemed so elegant, so…different from the very ordinary town in Ohio where I grew up."

"Aha," Gil said, "an Ohio native. I hear we get a few of you to cross the river and stay." Was that supposed to be a joke? Man, he was terrible at this.

"All the time I was growing up I wanted to move to Paris and open a shop. Something very elegant and very female and dripping in French sophistication." Her face changed a bit. "And then I met a man from Paris. But it was Paris, Kentucky. We talked about going to Paris, France, when we got married, but we could never afford it. And then we…ran out of time to go." He could see her force the sadness back down, push the thought away and drag herself into a new conversation. "How did you get the idea to start Homestretch Farm?"

"That's a long story for a place like this." And a very dangerous topic, despite the tender revelation she'd just offered. "The short version is that I wanted to make up for a few things. Give back."

"Meaning you could have used a place like Homestretch at some point? I mean, if that's not prying. It's no one's business why you do what you do."

Gil put down his fork. "Look, if you're wondering if my own record is squeaky clean, it ain't. You're not looking at a Boy Scout here."

There was another patch of silence as she considered that information. And he could tell by her face that she was giving it a lot of thought.

"Thanks," he said finally.

"For what?"

"For not pretending that was a small thing."

Emily gave him a confused look. "What do you mean?"

"I mean you can tell a lot about someone by how they react to that kind of information. The ones who gush and say things like 'it's not how you start, it's how you finish,' those are usually the people who'll quietly hold your record against you the rest of your life. The people who…I don't know…respect that for the admission it is, they're usually the ones you can trust."

She didn't ask for the details. He was glad of that, because he wasn't ready to give them. It wasn't exactly a topic of casual conversation, and they'd ventured deeper than he liked already. He changed the subject again. "So, Character Day. I'm not even sure I know what that is."

"It's one of those positive-reinforcement programs they have up at the high school. They take a month to focus on different positive character traits each week, and then there's an assembly thing where kids get awards for those traits. Students nominate each other. It's actually a pretty nice thing." She blushed.

"Sounds like it's an honor to be asked to speak."

"It is, sort of. It's supposed to hold you up as a—" she made quotation marks in the air with her fingers "'—Middleburgian of Character.'"

"You going to talk about what happened to your late husband?" No one had actually said that at the meeting, but he got the impression from the way people had acted. "I mean, I think that's really brave of you, if you are. It can't be easy."

Emily took a deep breath. "You know how Ash died?"

"Just the basics. You know, what people said or what was in the papers. I'm sorry."

She toyed with her pie for a moment. "Me, too. Ash was a good man."

"I've no doubt. You…you want to talk about it? I mean, I don't know the details and I don't need to, but if you want…" He couldn't think of a way to finish that sentence. "Well, you know, I'd listen." Gil wanted to smack his forehead for bumbling so much. He was so lousy at this kind of thing.

She gave a sad, thin smile. "Thanks, but it's a long story for a place like this."

"Yep," he said, putting more cream in his coffee just for something to do.

"But thanks," she said. "Really."

Gil found that despite the tangled conversation, they'd somehow managed to reach some sort of understanding. Both of them had uncomfortable baggage that didn't need unpacking just now. Could a conversation be classified as comfortably uncomfortable? "Still," he said, trying to perk up his voice a bit, "we got a challenge ahead of us, you and I. Don't you go caving when those guys come in there and try to get on your good side. They'll come up with eleven excuses for why they couldn't memorize this or they forgot that. Don't you fall for it. You've set your terms, now don't get all warm and fuzzy, y'hear? I don't want you to hand over one bar of soap that hasn't been duly earned."

She managed a smile. "I'll show no mercy."

"You stand your ground and hold the line."

She made a funny face and saluted him. "Yes, sir."

He saluted back. "I've a feeling my sanity depends on it."

Chapter Twelve

The shop-door chime rang and Peter Epson shuffled inside West of Paris. It was obvious Peter wasn't here to report—he had no notebook and didn't come straight to the counter. Instead, he wandered briefly around the shop, in that forced way of a customer hesitant to come out and ask for what he was truly seeking. Emily had grown to recognize this kind of "faux" browsing—mostly done by teenage girls looking for acne products and males of any age. She returned to arranging a display—such customers got prickly if you watched them too closely—and waited for him to speak up. Within a few minutes she found him nearly peering over her shoulder.

"I hear y'all got soap." He stuffed his hands in his pants pockets and smiled sheepishly. "Um…Love Soap?"

So word of the Edmundson's Fruits of the Spirit Soap had spread. Emily held up a bar of the love scent and nodded. "Yes, it just came in this month and it does smell wonderful." The soap had a thick, rosy aroma spiced through with something like chocolate.

Peter edged closer. "There's this girl…do you think…"

He rolled his eyes a bit and shrugged, which made him look excruciatingly young.

Emily leaned against the table. She loved this, guiding a customer to the perfect, heartfelt gift. She wasn't sure he wanted to know that she recognized him, so she simply met Peter's eyes with a warm smile. "She's special?"

"Yeah." He practically sighed and stubbed a toe on the floor. Dinah was right: a textbook case of puppy love, even at twenty.

"So you'd like something special for her? Something really nice?" She intentionally put the soap down and moved her hand toward a cream wool scarf on the next table. "Tell me about her and I'll help you pick something out."

He pointed to the Love Soap. "No, I pretty much just want that."

Emily raised a brow. "Have you been talking to the boys up at Homestretch Farm?" Well, it had to be asked, no matter how odd it sounded.

"No," he said, but in such a tone that she immediately knew he had. "Why would you ask that?"

"I think some people have the wrong idea about some of my soaps. I'd much rather we work together to come up with something she'd really like."

He picked the bar up off the counter. "I'm lousy at this. Maybe I should just stick with the soap."

"You just need a little help, that's all. A nice gift, if you present it with a bit of creativity, will definitely get her attention. Now, tell me what she's like."

Peter turned red. "She...um...brings the mail. Her birthday's today. And she has the most amazing hair."

"Peter," Emily said gently, deciding to acknowledge that she knew who he was, "are you sweet on Megan

Walters?" The cub reporter stuck on the town's newest mail carrier—could it get any more adorable? He nodded. "Well," Emily said, recalling Megan Walters's frenzied brown curls, "that she does. Relax, your secret's safe with me." She took the bar from his hands. "But I think she might like a few other things. Let's start with the soap and add some beautiful jeweled hairpins so she knows you like her hair. Valentine's Day is next week, you know."

"Yep."

Emily paused, thinking. "I've got an idea that should sweep her off her feet, Peter. Come on over here and let's get planning."

Back in Five Minutes the sign read.

Who leaves their shop? Then again, how should he know? He'd never even darkened the door of West of Paris before this month. Now, it seemed as if every third errand took him past the place. Maybe she left all the time to run errands or handle bath-product crises. He looked over into the small alley beside her shop and could see the blue fender of her VW. She hadn't gone very far. He turned and scanned up and down the street.

Five blocks down, at what looked like the corner of March Avenue, he thought he saw her white beret. She had one of those baskets at her feet and she kept reaching into it for things.

Before he even had a chance to think about it, he started walking down Ballad Road toward the corner where Emily stood.

He didn't know what to say when he got close enough to see her task. She was tying a little gift bag—a yellow one from her shop—to…a mailbox.

A mailbox?

He watched her for a second or two, but she was so engrossed in making little strips of newspaper curl like ribbons that she didn't see him behind her. He shifted his weight and leaned down to peer at her face—he had a good foot and a half on her, even bent over like that. "For crying out loud, what are you doing?"

Emily jumped, sending her scissors clean through the paper she was trying to curl. "Thanks a lot. Now I've gone and cut it off and I only have one more." She made a little humphing noise and began to dig into that basket of hers.

"Sorry, but what exactly is it you need one more of and why?"

She eyed him, scissors poised midair. "That information is on a need-to-know basis, and you have no basis or business knowing."

"You're tying things to a mailbox."

She turned her attention back to her work. "Very observant, Mr. Sorrent."

"You know you can call me Gil," he corrected, trying to ignore how much he liked their banter.

"Yes, *Gil,* I am tying something to a mailbox." She kept her eyes on her task, as if that statement should have closed the matter.

But it didn't. People didn't decorate mailboxes. Well, *normal* people didn't decorate mailboxes. "It's weird."

"Weird or not, it's not your business."

That struck him as odd. Given the circumstances, he would think someone as precise as Emily Montague would be eager to explain her unusual behavior. But she was quiet. Secretive, even. He caught a whiff of something in the air, then pointed at the bag. "Is that *soap* in there?"

She didn't answer.

"Why are you tying soap to the mailbox?"

She turned on him, drawing herself up to as tall as she got—which wasn't that tall, actually—and lowering her voice to a growl. "This is the private request of a particular customer—and yes, I tried to talk him out of it—but no, I'm not going to tell you a thing."

He pointed at her. "Ha! So it's a 'he.'" A frightening thought struck him. "It had better not be one of my guys, I'll tell you that. Cuz you can just pick up your things and go home if it is."

"Could you just *once* stop jumping to conclusions and telling me what to do?" She adjusted the decorations around the bag, checked her watch—why did she check her watch?—and thrust her supplies back into the basket. "It's not one of your guys, so there."

He looked a little more closely at the odd packaging. She'd used red ribbon and strips of newspaper, of all things. "You run out of ribbon or something? That's newspaper."

"Again, very observant. Yes, I'm quite aware I've used newspaper. And, again, I'm not going to tell you why." She checked her watch again. "Come on, we have to get out of here, it's nearly time." She started back up the street toward her shop.

"Time for what? What's going on?"

She spun back around. "Don't you dare stick around to find out. Leave her be, you understand me?" She gave him a fierce look and started walking again.

He started after her, completely stumped. "Her? Who?"

"Nope," she called over her shoulder.

"Then maybe I'll just stand here till I find out." He could never seem to let her have the last word.

"You will not."

"I could."

"You wouldn't," she said.

"Who's stopping me?"

"I am. And your sense of honor."

Well, now, that was dirty pool. How, by any stretch of the imagination, could it be a matter of honor that he leave a bar of soap dangling from a mailbox in privacy? "Honor's got nothin' to do with this."

"Well, I'd appeal to your sense of romance, but seeing as you have none…"

"I…" That should go challenged somehow, but Gil was hanged if he knew how. "I do, too." *Oh, brilliant,* he thought to himself. *Mud could have come up with better than that, and he's a dog.*

"Then leave them be." Emily looked back over her shoulder, checked her watch another time, and made a herding motion with her hand to hurry him up the block before whatever it was that was supposed to happen took place.

They walked for a few steps, her shorter legs working to keep up with his long strides. He noticed she had a lacy white scarf to match her fuzzy beret. With her face surrounded by all that frothy white, her eyes stood out in contrast. Hazel wasn't really a stand-out eye color, normally, but her eyes had a clear, shiny quality surrounded by all that softness. He'd known her for months—maybe even seen her around town for years—but he'd never noticed that before.

Gil kept glancing over his shoulder as they made their way down the street. Just as they reached West of Paris, Megan Walters turned the corner in her postal uniform.

And he realized who the soap was for. "She's here," he warned. He and Emily scurried into the small alcove made by her shop entryway and peeked back.

"No, don't," Emily said, tugging on his coat sleeve, but she didn't really mean it. He knew she couldn't help herself from watching.

Megan stared at the mailbox for a long time, glancing around before peering at the package. Her body language made it obvious when she realized the package was for her, even from this distance. "Who's it from?" Gil asked quietly, noticing how Emily's head fit under his chin as they peered around the corner.

"I'm not telling," she whispered, tilting her head back around a bit to see him. Her eyes seemed to have six different colors in them, not just hazel.

Megan pulled the soap out of the bag and held it to her face. *She's smelling it,* he thought. *Why is everyone in Middleburg suddenly smelling things?* Emily smelled nice. "Does *she* know who it's from?"

"You don't get to know," Emily said, her voice more playful. Gil could tell she was getting a huge kick out of watching Megan, even though he was sure she'd never admit to it even if he pressed her. Megan pulled something shiny out of the bag, then looked up the street toward the shop. Emily and Gil ducked back quickly into the alcove so as not to be seen.

It made Emily laugh.

It made Gil feel idiotic. A grown man ducking into corners like a prank-pulling schoolboy.

"So what did I just watch?" he said, trying to sound as if the current situation was completely normal. "Patience? Kindness? Pirate?"

"No," Emily said, trying to sound conversational, but completely failing to keep that girly, dreamy quality out of her voice. "Love."

"Love Soap."

"Love Soap," she repeated, still trying to sound businesslike.

As he followed her into the store, Gil decided there just wasn't a way to say "Love Soap" in a businesslike manner. Gil just didn't get the whole scented soap thing to begin with. He didn't know how to make heads or tails of what he just saw, and it was driving him crazy. He stood for a moment, watching her put away the basket of supplies she'd used to decorate Megan's gift, then abruptly snagged a bar of the Gentleness Soap off the table. He sniffed it, then wrinkled up his nose at the smell. *You can't smell gentle. You just can't.* She laughed at the face he made. "All right, I give up. I don't get it. I saw Megan's face, I saw your face, but I still don't get it. It's just soap. Men don't care about this kind of stuff and I just don't get what's so special about it."

"I'm not sure I can explain it. It's not the kind of thing you can easily put into words." She considered him for a moment, then reached for a nearby stool. "Take off your coat and come over here." She turned her shop's Open sign back to Closed again.

"What?"

"I can only think of one way to explain this to you, and you're going to have to sit right here for it to work."

Gil looked highly suspicious. She had to point to the small stool a second time before he settled his large frame onto it. His knees practically came up to his chest, but he managed to park his elbows on them and shift his weight a bit. "What're you gonna do?" Emily just smiled at him.

Chapter Thirteen

"Close your eyes." A tiny curl of enjoyment let loose in Emily's stomach. She'd never tried to explain the power of scent before—at least not to someone who didn't get it already. Certainly never to someone as clearly resistant as Gil Sorrent.

"You're not gonna put anything on me, are you?" He gave her a look as if to suggest that contact with hand cream might melt the skin off his bones.

"I'm not going to do anything of the sort. But if you close your eyes, you'll find it easier to concentrate on your sense of smell."

He stared at her, then closed his eyes, only to pop them warily back open a second later. His glare was half caution, half annoyance.

"It won't hurt," she teased.

"That's not what I'm afraid of," he muttered as he closed his eyes and flexed his fingers against his knees.

Best to start with something familiar. Emily picked up his leather coat, which he'd parked on the floor by the table. It was thick and soft, and her fingers touched the inside collar when she picked it up—it was still warm from his neck. "This is your coat. All leather has a smell, and lots of times it's distinct to each thing. Can you smell it?" She held the coat up to his face and watched his brows wrinkle up as he inhaled. "It's probably familiar, so you might have to work at it a bit at first." He was trying. Feeling a bit foolish, maybe, but trying. "What does it smell like to you?"

Gil opened one eye. "It smells like a coat."

"But what does *your* coat smell like? Horses? Saddle soap? Hay?"

Gil closed his eyes and made a big show out of sniffing his coat. It made her laugh. "Hate to break it to you, but all I smell is my coat."

Maybe familiar wasn't the way to go. "Let's try something else." She selected the Peace Soap and held it toward him. "See if you can name anything you smell. The sense of smell is fully developed in us from birth, and is one of the last to leave us in death. Babies can smell their mothers just hours after they're born, you know."

"Anyone who's ever spent time near a barn won't argue with you about the power of smell."

"I'm not talking about powerful smells, I'm talking about the power of scent. They're different things." Emily waved the soap near his face. "Aromas have been known to shift emotions, evoke memories and even bring about chemical changes in your body. Like how you get hungry when you smell ham cooking."

"That's it, cooking," Gil ventured. "It's kind of a baking smell."

"See? You *can* smell things. That's vanilla. Very

calming, mostly because we associate it with home. What else?" She watched his eyes shift and search beneath closed lids. He had long, thick lashes.

"There's more in there?" Ever the skeptic.

"Yep. See if you can find it."

He shifted slightly toward her on the stool. She noticed his corduroy shirt had a button missing up by the collar. It had the uneven, worn color of a man who didn't take much care with his laundry. "Flowers. Something flowery. Girly—well, sorry, but that's the word that came to mind."

"Lavender. See? You *can* pick it out. And yes, it's considered very feminine. Both lavender and vanilla are calming scents, so you can see why they've put them in the Peace Soap. There's one more note, though, so see if you can pick it out."

"Note?" He started to open his eyes.

"Keep those shut." Emily put her hand to his shoulder before she realized it, and the contact did something to her she wasn't ready to admit. She pulled her hand away, but not before she saw his whole body react. "We identify scents by calling them notes." She continued, more formally. "You'll hear people use that term when they talk about wine or perfume."

"Or soap." His voice was so low it rumbled through her.

"C'mon," she said, thankful he couldn't see how flustered she felt, "play along here."

He took a moment, searching for the scent. "Um…nuts of some kind?"

Emily smiled. "Almond. See? You're good at this."

"Don't let that get out," he said, and opened his eyes. When he did, she felt as if she ought to back up ten steps. They were a little too close. He knew it, too—she could tell by the way he shot up off the stool. "I'm pretty much a Pine-Sol kind of guy and I think I'd like to keep it that way."

"You like pie, right? A huge part of how we taste is connected to our sense of smell. No shame in that."

"Apple pie is one thing. Lavender vanilla whatever is a whole other ball of wax. If I used that out on the farm, I'd never hear the end of it."

Emily put a hand on one hip. "There's a whole ball of wax between a good-smelling man and one doused with bad cologne, too, so don't write off scent so quickly, mister."

"Exactly," he said, pointing at her. "There's *scented* and then there's *smelly*. Perfume's perfume. Why's soap got to smell like anything but soap?" He picked up the bar she held. "I can't believe this stuff's any better than plain soap."

"Not all soap is created equal." Emily adjusted the cardboard list of Bible verses she'd propped up on a tiny white easel behind the Fruits of the Spirit soaps. "But it was more than just quality soap. I liked the idea. You know, the Bible verses on the labels. It's unique." She caught Gil's face and added, "Okay, maybe *odd,* but you gotta admit it's a clever way to get a bit of scripture into someone's hands."

Gil squared off with her. "You know what guys look for in soap?"

"What's that?"

"Soap." He chuckled, and for a moment she saw his laugh light up shades of topaz inside the dark brown of his eyes. Just a moment, though—a fraction of a second before he looked away and reached for his coat. "Well, thanks for the lesson. Can't say as I get it any better than before, but, well, you tried."

"So you won't be joining the ranks of Homestretch Farm Pirate Soap customers?" she teased.

"Actually, I have to, don't I? Gotta keep my end of the

deal, since you got on the horse." He pulled out his wallet. "Three bars of the smelliest stuff you got. I believe that was our bargain."

"You remembered. Yes, well, I've been thinking about that. I could give you something so full of scent you're likely to hide it away in your barn, but I'd much rather sell you something you might actually use."

He cast her a doubtful glance, as if the possibility of her having anything he would actually use was mighty slim. "You'd have to look pretty hard to find somethin'. No offense."

Emily reached into a counter drawer and pulled out three square bars wrapped in brown paper. "This is gardening soap. It has a scent, but not one likely to send you running. It's meant for working hands. There's things in here to get a lot of grime off your hands, to remove plant oils, and some protective elements to keep your hands from drying out. Functional all the way. Think of it as hand cleanser in solid form." She handed him the trio of bars. Much like the Pirate Soap, they had decidedly rugged packaging. "But they're two dollars more per bar than the Edmundson's, so there's a definite trade-off."

He gave a broad, genuine smile. "You do like to cut a deal, don't you? Six extra dollars to not smell like a perfume bottle? I suppose that's fair." He held up a hand. "But I'm makin' no promises to actually use the stuff. I said I'd buy it, I never said I'd use it."

"Fair's fair," Emily said, smiling to herself as she rang up the sale. The register's *ching* sounded particularly victorious on this transaction.

Gil put his coat on. "I got to get to lunch. I always eat late to miss the lunch rush at the Grill."

Emily raised an eyebrow. "This is Middleburg, Kentucky. We don't have a lunch rush."

And there it was—an actual full-fledged laugh from Gil Sorrent. She found she very much liked the sound. When he looked back up at her, the topaz had returned full-force to his eyes.

Emily recounted her last two visits with Gil Sorrent as she and Sandy stuffed envelopes for a church mailing that night. They were the only two volunteers who showed up, so it was the perfect chance for a private chat about her growing fascination with Homestretch Farm and its surprising owner.

"Well, he looks like the gizmo type to me," Sandy agreed after Emily described the session in Gil's office. "He's always flipping his cell phone open or that little black doodad of his to make notes or appointments. And his truck looks like it has every option known to man. Why is it men think we're all impressed by how complicated they can make things? George put in a new computer system in the stores, and he spent months yapping at me about how it would make life easier. That man ought to have been married long enough to me to know I don't trust all them fancy machines. So you can imagine my surprise," she said as she laid a hand across her chest in mock drama, reaching for another stack of envelopes, "when it's been nothing but trouble. I can hardly sell a pair of socks without something flashin' 'Error' somewhere and beeping all over the place."

Emily laughed. She could just picture the kind of talking-to Sandy would give a malfunctioning machine. But she couldn't imagine Sandy's long pink fingernails making friends with any kind of keyboard. George had one long uphill battle ahead of him, that's for sure. "Well, you already know how far I keep from electronics, but I have to say I was impressed. He's done some pretty amazing things with the technology out on the farm."

"Honey, will you think for a minute about what you just said? 'Technology out on the farm?' Sound like one of them oxymorons to you?"

Emily thought about it for a moment. "I thought so at first, but I suppose it makes sense. Farming's a business like any other—technology could be a help."

"Assuming, of course, that the stuff actually works." Sandy shot Emily a knowing glance over her envelopes. "And my goodness, when did you soften up your stance on software? I do recall havin' to harp on you even to get a cell phone." She gathered up her envelopes and began tapping them into a neat stack. "Oh, it's obvious Gil Sorrent's made an impression on you, bless your heart. But it ain't the normal kind of electricity we're talkin' about here."

Emily cringed. She'd gone out of her way not to color her description with anything that might tip Sandy off to the insistent spark of attraction she was feeling for Gil. She should have known it was a lost cause—hiding that kind of stuff from Sandy was impossible. The woman had abilities the FBI couldn't match. "Okay, I admit I may have…*adjusted* my opinion of him."

"Adjusted?" Sandy raised one perfectly waxed eyebrow. "What kind of fool do you take me for?" She put down the stack. "Emily, hon, why are you treating this like it's some kind of disease? I'm glad for you. Baffled, but glad. I didn't picture the two of you gettin' on well at all."

"But Sandy—"

Sandy rolled her eyes. "So he's a bit of a sourpuss, but there's evidently a nice guy hiding under all that grumbling. He's single, he's a man of faith and he's not so hard on the eyes. And as for the herd of hoodlums, well, all men come with some kind of baggage, honey, even the ones who look like they don't."

Emily allowed herself a tiny smile. "He has such a passion for what he does."

"That's a good thing. Not too many men willing to put it on the line for something like that." Sandy softened her voice to a whisper and reached out to touch Emily's arm. "It's time, Emily girl, it's more than time. You been alone long enough. Even Ash wouldn't begrudge you finding happiness again."

Emily couldn't form a reply. It'd been years since a man kindled a little bit of anything in her, despite Sandy's many attempts to set her up. But that was just the thing—Sandy would have never tried to fix her up with someone like Gil. He was so far from her idea of the right man. The whole thing had caught her off guard. And there was still so much she didn't know about him. Like why he was so dark and hard and sullen. But there was something else in there, too. Something she guessed he didn't show often or easily. It would slip out in a word or a look when she was around, and he always seemed just as surprised to reveal it as she was to discover it. Something seemed to click when they were together, even though they both had pieces of their past they weren't yet willing to share.

"I'm not sure I'm ready," she said after a long pause.

"Who's ever ready? No one said you have to marry the man by sundown. Start out with a dinner or something. There ain't a deadline involved."

Emily wasn't sure she'd ever be ready. Her heart already had a wound in it a mile long. Could Gil Sorrent be the man to heal that wound? Or would he just be the man to deepen it?

Chapter Fourteen

Very young customers—usually a staple around Mother's Day—were among Emily's favorites. So Emily could barely contain her amusement when a very serious nine-year-old Tommy Lee Lockwood came into the shop. He marched straight up to the counter and asked for a bar of Edmundson's Self-Control Soap. "I got my four dollars right here." He reached into his pocket and pulled out four wadded-up dollar bills, along with three marbles and two baseball cards. "Daddy said if Mama don't quit smoking soon, he don't know what he'll do, so I want to buy her this. I heard him saying last week that all she needed was self-control. And I heard you got some."

Emily wasn't entirely sure what to do with that state-ment. "I got all kinds of nice things for mamas. And you're sweet for wanting to help your mama do something so im-portant. She's lucky to have you."

"You got any math smarts soap? I could use that if it works."

Now Tommy Lee wasn't all wrong: scents like grapefruit and bergamot were often energizing, and they could produce feelings of capability and were often attributed to clarity of thought. But math aptitude and self-control weren't coming to him or his mama by way of a long hot bath with the right soap. "Where'd you get the idea that soap could help you with math, Tommy Lee?"

"Around," he said, looking away.

Emily could just guess around *where*.

"What is 'roman therapy,' anyways? Sounds kooky."

"It's 'aromatherapy,' and it can make you feel calmer or more energetic but it can't help your mama do something as important as quit smoking." She saw Tommy Lee's expression fall. "But you can help lots of other ways. You can encourage her and help her feel nice while she's working so hard to quit. It's really hard to do, did you know that? And you're a smart man for coming to the store today because I'm having a very special sale. Your four dollars is going to go a long way. How about we make her up a basket of things to help her feel pretty?"

The spark returned to his big blue eyes.

Halfway through the gathering of a basket worth about four times as much as she was going to charge him, Emily looked at Tommy Lee. "Does your daddy know where you are?"

"He thinks I'm at the bakery with Miss Hopkins. He got into a big ol' discussion with the bad-man-farm man while we were down at the hardware store."

"The bad-man-farm man"? Emily had to think a moment. She didn't like what came to her. "You mean Mr. Sorrent from Homestretch Farm?"

Tommy Lee gave her a blank look.

"Tall, dark, brown leather coat, kinda grumpy?"

"Yep."

"How about I just call over there and let your daddy know you're with me while you decide which color ribbon we should use." She pointed to a spool of several ribbon colors while she called Gil's cell phone.

Gil and Matt Lockwood came in just as Emily was tying off the last ribbon on the basket. Tommy Lee insisted on showing it off to the men, and Emily watched in amusement as Gil hunkered down on one knee and let that little boy show him every item in the basket. The dad tolerated the little demonstration, but Gil listened as though Tommy Lee were showing him the coolest new gadgets. He even asked a few questions and made a point of congratulating Tommy Lee on making a good purchase.

What impressed Emily most was the fact that Gil made a fuss over that little boy with an armful of "smelly stuff" after talking with Matt Lockwood, who evidently referred to Homestretch as "the bad-man farm." It made Emily wonder how many little digs like that Gil Sorrent endured in a week.

"How are you gonna stay in business if you sell expensive baskets like that for four dollars?" Gil said as he watched Tommy Lee wobble down street with the enormous gift.

"I couldn't help indulging him. He came in here looking for the Self-Control Soap to help his mama quit smoking. Isn't that the sweetest thing?"

"I heard the whole story. In detail," Gil said, with the tone of a man who'd just been treated to more detail than he would have liked, "You mind telling me what exactly self-control *smells* like?"

"Bergamot," Emily said, smoothing out the crumpled dollar bills as she slid them into the cash register along with a marble Tommy Lee gave her as a tip for the gift wrap. "It's mostly bergamot and grapefruit, with a bit of mint."

"Grapefruit? You gotta be kidding me."

"No, really, citrus has a very cleansing effect on most people. Very energizing. Clarity of thought. That kind of thing. Makes sense when you think about what makes up self-control."

He looked straight at her. "You really believe all this aroma nonsense? That smelling something affects how anybody feels and acts?"

She'd been waiting for him to ask her that. Seen the question festering behind his eyes since that day she'd asked him to describe how his coat smelled. "Feels, yes. But acts? No. I believe scent affects people. It changes how we view a room, how we taste food, how we remember a moment. It affects us as much as sight and touch, or sound." She reached for a stack of scented shelf liners, wanting to shift her gaze off his face. "I've never really understood why people give smelling something less importance than hearing music or seeing a sunset. It's a sense, like the other four, but it gets the short shrift, if you ask me."

"Well, I do admit to caring a lot about how things taste, that's true. And Paulo tells me I don't care near enough about how I look, but then I'd say Paulo cares way too much, so we're even there." Gil crossed his arms and leaned back against her counter. It was the first time Emily thought he looked anything near comfortable in her store. The hard edge was gone, and the set of his shoulders wasn't so tense. She knew he was somewhere in his late thirties, but his face had the texture of a hard life about it. Dark lines and rough patches. It had made him look older at first, but not so much now.

"But the soap," he said taking a step toward her. "I'm talking about smells changing things. Altering things."

"You mean do I believe it can bring love or joy or peace or patience? No, I don't believe that. I don't believe it can transform a person." She hesitated briefly before adding, "I think only the Holy Spirit can make that kind of change." She looked at him. "You didn't think because I bought all that soap that I...?"

He stared at her. "No, but I just needed to hear you say it." Gil ran his finger down the side of a vase sitting on a nearby shelf. "So, what about you? I mean, if you think scent affects people, what kind of soap do you use?" He suddenly looked embarrassed, as though he hadn't meant to ask such a highly personal question.

It felt highly personal, but was it? Was it any different than asking a mechanic what kind of car he drove? Emily tried to tell herself it wasn't a personal question as she felt a blush color her cheeks. "Well," she started, trying to sound technical, "as you'd expect, I change it a lot. Depending on what suits me any given day."

Gil tucked one hand into his back pocket. Either he had no idea of the depth of what he was asking, or he hid it in the name of curiosity. "Surely you've got favorites. I mean you must really like the stuff."

"I do. Have favorites, I mean. I always try things before I sell them in the shop, too."

"Unless it's Pirate Soap," he reminded her.

"Yes, well, I reckon that'll go down as the biggest whopping mistake in Emily Montague history."

Gil scratched his chin. "You could do worse."

Of course, the owner of the Homestretch Farm rehabilitation program for offenders would be highly aware of what qualified as life's whopping big mistakes, wouldn't he? "I suppose you're right," Emily said. She picked up a bottle of peach-cream bubble bath. "This is a personal favorite sure to wrinkle the nose of any rugged American male." She unscrewed the cap off the tester bottle and handed it to him.

He sniffed it and frowned. "Do you eat this or bathe in it?" He put the bottle down quickly. "Why is it women think men like their women to smell like food? Men like food to smell like food, and women to smell like women."

"Oh, is *that* why you think we do it? For your benefit?" She quickly added, "I mean, speaking of the female and male populations as a whole. You think we use scent only to get men?"

Gil clammed up, looking as though he'd decided there was no safe way to answer that question. He was right, and she made sure her glare let him know it. "Women use scent because *we* like it. Because we recognize the effect it has on *us*. It's an enhancement."

"So which 'enhancement' is your favorite, aside from that peachy stuff? You don't always smell like food, so they're not all fruity like that."

He hadn't even realized what he'd said. He'd just given away far more than he knew, because by admitting that he knew she didn't always smell like peach, he just admitted that he knew what she *did* smell like. That he could recognize her scent. "Could you pick it out? Can your high-tech brain meet such a low-tech challenge?" Emily asked, smiling.

"Is that a dare?" he said with a very particular tone in his voice.

"It's on that table over there." Emily told herself to wipe the smirk off her face as she pointed to a display of hand lotions. Somehow, she knew he'd get it. He'd know which. She'd be able to see it on his face, and she was unsure what that moment would do to her.

He walked cautiously over to the table, scanned the collection, and picked up the rose-scented bottle. He sniffed it, ran his finger around the top of the bottle for some reason, then set it down. Emily shifted her feet and coughed, suddenly unable to find anything to do with her hands. Why on earth was she behaving this way? Why did this man drive her to impulsive acts she'd surely regret?

Gil tested a second bottle—a sandalwood-almond scent—and although he had to sniff it a second time, he put it down, as well.

He picked up a patchouli-rosewood blend, one she knew was the correct choice. Oh, my. She was right. She could tell the moment he recognized it. His whole body changed, and it sent a jolt down through her toes. The moment caught them both by surprise, although he hid it better than she suspected she did.

He walked back over to the counter and put the bottle between them. "*That's* you," he said softly.

When he looked up at her, she knew he could sense it as much as she could. *It.* The simmering tug when they were together. That thing that made her look twice as long as she ought to, that made her remember what his jacket smelled like and how his shirt collar never did stay down on one side. "That's you," he said again.

Emily waited a long moment before she nodded, mostly because she knew that her nod meant much more than just acknowledging his correct choice of bottles. "My favorite," she said quietly, and she saw something kindle in the depth of his eyes.

Just then a cluster of teenage girls burst into the store, ending the moment with a storm of noisy giggles and activity.

Emily couldn't say if she was mad at or grateful for the interruption.

Chapter Fifteen

Gil usually enjoyed stacking hay. It was hard, honest work a man felt down to his bones. Of course, that was probably when it was necessary work. Right now, it was more like he was rearranging hay. But he needed something physically hard to do, and there weren't a lot of those kinds of tasks on the farm this time of year. He figured a good half an hour moving big, awkward objects might shake the willies out of him and help him think.

After the hay had been rearranged, and rearranged, Gil resorted to wandering among the stalls. He did some of his best thinking—and his most fervent praying—near the animals. They had that effect on people; gently imploring eyes, subtle movements, huffs of breath that sounded like sighs. Nobody begged to be petted in a stable; they just seemed to stand there and listen. It worked calm into a soul. A calm that was one of the basic principles of Homestretch Farm.

It wasn't like he didn't know what was eating at him, making him restless. He did. He just didn't know what to do about it.

He knew the basic story of Emily's husband's death. Talented local man heads off to the big city to further his career only to find himself in the wrong place at the wrong time. It had never surprised him that she'd been opposed to Homestretch Farm three years ago. She had a right to be wary of criminals. Her suspicion didn't bother him at all.

It was people like Matt Lockwood, Tommy Lee's dad, who drove him crazy. Those people pretended tolerance, pretended to support Homestretch Farm, but deep down wished it would go away. Did Matt really think Gil didn't know Tommy Lee called it "the bad-man farm"? Did Matt think Gil had any doubts about who taught him to call it that?

That was the difference between people like Matt and people like Emily. Matt would always pretend but never change his mind. Emily had never pretended. If he had changed her mind—and he believed he had—it was because he'd earned it.

Supporting the farm was one thing. On a more personal level—and it was growing more personal by the day—Gil didn't think Emily would be able to deal with his past. *Is this Your idea of justice, Lord? I finally find someone I want to be able to forgive my history, and it's the woman in Middleburg most hurt by crime?*

Romeo nuzzled at Gil's jacket, obviously remembering where he usually tucked a carrot when he came out to the stables. "No goodies today, boy." He picked up a brush and began working over the horse's gleaming coat, more for something to occupy his hands than for any grooming need. *I'm lonely, Lord. I wouldn't let myself admit it before now, but I'm lonely.* It didn't help matters one bit that tomorrow was Valentine's Day.

Across the stall, Lady Macbeth whinnied and stomped,

jealous of the attention Romeo was getting. "What's with you, 'Beth? You lonely, too?" Lady Macbeth had been a risky purchase. She'd been abused as a young horse, and for months was skittish around people. Gil couldn't let the less-experienced hands near her for the first year. Now, with two years of love and care, Lady Macbeth had become one of the gentlest horses on the farm, and a shameless flirt, besides. He'd known he could trust her to do right by Emily. Gil had a special soft spot for 'Beth, because he loved risks that paid off.

Valentine's Day. The house seemed dark and far too big. Even after four years, this day was just plain hard. Ash had made it so special each year that the day itself just seemed to magnify his absence. She imagined it was a hard day for anyone who was alone, but having known such loving, romantic celebrations of the holiday seemed to make it worse. It was a blessing of sorts that West of Paris was always busy right down to the last minute. A bath shop was a major destination for panicked men on Valentine's Day, and she'd spent every one of the last four years glad for a reason to keep the store open late. Sandy joked that Emily saved a dozen marriages a year by staying open and helping last-minute shoppers.

Once the key was turned and the shop lights were out, however, it was a hollow satisfaction.

Emily puttered around the house for a few hours, too restless to go to bed early, too blue to call anyone for company. It wasn't until nearly eleven that Emily remembered it was Tuesday. Which meant it was pie night at Deacon's Grill. A walk to Deacon's was just the kind of diversion she needed. She could even have a slice at the diner, and take another home for a decadent breakfast. Confident that she had the perfect plan, Emily snagged her hat and house key, and headed out the door.

She had forgotten—or maybe just blocked out— Deacon's other Tuesday-night regular. Gil was just settling down to a mile-high slice of lemon meringue when Emily walked in. Well, of course he'd be here. Hadn't he been the one to let her in on the Tuesday-night secret of Deacon's?

"A new Tuesday-night regular, are we?" he joked as she slipped onto a stool two away from his at the counter. He took a huge bite of his pie. "Ahh. I told you it was worth it."

Emily was just about to go into some explanation as to why she had nothing better to do on Valentine's Day then eat pie in a diner when the door opened behind her. In walked Peter Epson and Megan Walters, looking supremely lovestruck.

Gil leaned toward Emily with a smart-aleck look plastered on his face. "Isn't that a certain mail carrier?"

"Hush," Emily chided him, amazed that the entire diner didn't erupt in "aww"s as Peter pulled out Megan's chair at a corner table. "Don't you dare say anything, Gil. Not a word."

By this time Peter had excused himself and strutted— yes, that was most definitely a strut—over to Emily.

"It worked," he whispered with glee. "Wow."

Gil looked like he had a dozen opinions on that, but Emily ignored him. "The gift certainly caught Megan's eye, hmm?"

"Yep," he said in a distracted tone as he stared back over his shoulder at Megan. She waved. He sighed.

Gil choked on his coffee.

"I think she likes you," Emily whispered.

"Yeah," Peter beamed. "I think so. But she's *so* perfect. I don't think she'd have looked at me before."

"She's lookin' at you now, that's for sure," Gil cut in. "That girl's hung up something fierce on you."

"Maybe she is." Peter said it like it was the most unlikely thing in the universe. "Wow."

"Wow, indeed," Emily replied. "Now go wow *her* and stop talking to *me*."

Gil leaned in and nudged Peter. "You leave a pretty gal alone like that on Valentine's Day and there's no telling what could happen." Peter erupted in an awkward, almost teenage laugh. "No, really," Gil said with a bit more emphasis, "you *need* to get over there."

"Oh, yeah, right, I suppose I should." He gave Gil an us-men-know-all-about-that-kind-of-stuff grin and strutted back to his newfound lady love.

Gil stared after him. "Tell me I was never that young."

Emily couldn't help but smile. "We were all that young once." When Gil shot her a look, she added, "Okay, maybe some of us were more subtle about it than others."

"Everyone's more subtle than Peter. He tied soap to a mailbox. I had him pegged for smarter than that." Gil shook his head and returned to his pie.

Emily turned to him. "I'm the one who tied that soap to a mailbox, I'll remind you. And it clearly did the trick." He gave her a non-committal grunt. "Come on, you can't tell me you never did anything dumb when you were young?"

He stopped with his fork in midair. "I never said that." He kept his fork still, as if he hadn't finished his thought.

He looked at her out of the corner of his eye and said quietly, "I think we can all agree that 'accessory to felony' rates as highly stupid."

Felony. Serious crime. His insight into the guys and how they ended up where they were came from personal experience. He'd told her as much the last time they were in here. It shouldn't have surprised her, but it did. He seemed like such a man of principle. Then again, some people come by their principles the hard way.

Megan's giggle caught their attention. She had evidently dropped her napkin, and Peter was picking it back up for her like a chivalrous knight. When he dabbed at a bit of blueberry pie on her cheek, it was comically romantic. All that gooey innocence was amusing but a bit hard to bear after a point.

"Even though the show of lovebirds is mighty entertaining, I'm afraid it's getting late," Gil said and pulled a few bills from his wallet, laying them on the counter.

Emily checked her watch. "Goodness, you're right— who knew I'd be walking home after midnight on Valentine's Day?"

Gil stopped cold. "You walked here? At this time of night? Alone?"

Emily didn't take to the overprotective tone of his voice. "It's three blocks, and I know every single house on the way. It's a small town and I'm a big girl." She paid up, as well, forgetting about the second piece of pie for a decadent breakfast.

"Not gonna happen."

"Pardon?"

"I'm walking you home. Even if I have to follow you in my truck twenty feet back going two miles an hour. I don't care how big you are or how small this town is." He squared his shoulders and suddenly there was the gruff Gil Sorrent she'd known—the human fortress of opinions not open to debate.

Without a word, he opened the door for her and she walked out into the snowy night.

Chapter Sixteen

She was out of her mind even to think of walking home alone at this hour. He'd have insisted on escorting *any* woman in that situation, but with Emily it was absolutely non-negotiable. He'd see her home and there was no point in arguing.

The sky was a bit cloudy, with snow sparkling through the pools of moonlight. A snowflake landed on her eyelash, and she fished that ridiculously fuzzy beret out of her coat pocket and put it on. "Fine. If we're going to walk, let's at least enjoy it. It's a beautiful night, and some of us know how to appreciate beauty." She gestured up toward the ornate streetlights that lined the sidewalk. He wouldn't admit it, but he'd revised his earlier opinion of them. They were fussy, but they did add atmosphere.

"Aren't they charming? Worth the extra money?"

"I didn't much take to them at first."

"Oh, I noticed," she said. "One thing I can say about you, Gil Sorrent—you know how to argue your point."

"I thought Middleburg had better places to put its money."

"And now?"

"Can we leave the civic budget for another night?"

"Fine by me." She ran her bare hand along a fence, brushing the snow off as they walked past.

"Didn't you bring any gloves? Or those fuzzy mittens you're always wearing?"

She smiled. "I must have been in such a hurry for pie I forgot them. It's not that cold out."

He pulled his gloves off and handed them to her. "Here, take mine. I'm fine without them."

She started to protest, and he shot her a look. Sighing, she put her hands into the large gloves and flopped the nearly empty fingers at him. "All safe and warm now, okay?"

It really wasn't that far to her frosted-cupcake house. The place looked postcard pretty in the moonlight. Gingerbread latticework collected an icing of snow on the corners of her roof. Pale-green shutters hugged each of the multipaned windows and a red-heart wreath hung on the front door. The white picket fence around her yard was the finishing touch, making the house look like it belonged on a calendar page. "Your house suits you," he offered.

"I love this house. Your office suits you, you know."

Another reminder of how different they were. He turned up his coat collar. His hair was practically standing on end, but it had nothing to do with the cold. He unlatched her gate for her.

She looked up at him as she walked through. Another snowflake settled onto her cheek, and he fought the urge to brush it away before it melted. "You were nice to walk me home. I'm sorry I put up such a fuss. You get enough from other people in the town—I don't need to add to it."

"What do you mean?"

"Let's just say *I* don't think of Homestretch as 'the bad-man farm.'" She caught his eye with a warm smile before she reached into her coat pocket and pulled out her keys. Her smile uncurled something deep in his chest.

"You used to," Gil said.

"You're right," she admitted, walking up her front steps. "I wasn't a big fan at first." She turned to face him. "But I've changed my mind. You do fine things up there."

Emily had a gift for saying things that made it hard for Gil to keep a safe distance. That woman looked so soft for someone who'd had a hard lot in life. She must have tremendous faith to be able to keep from being bitter about all that had happened to her. There was a part of him that wanted to ask her about that—here, in the middle of the night—but he knew that would be a dangerous place to go. Right now, just being with her felt dangerous. He knew that if he stayed much longer, that safe distance would be come impossible.

"Well now, you're home safe and sound."

"Thanks to you. My hero." She fumbled with her keys in the great big gloves.

Why do they always fiddle with their keys? Don't women know what it does to us when they stand at the door and fiddle with their keys? He brushed the comment away. "Anyone would have done the same. Matter of honor and all."

"You're coming to the Character Day thing on Thursday, aren't you? All of the town council was invited."

He knew he was invited, he just didn't think the owner of Homestretch Farm ought to show up to Character Day. It felt a bit ironic to him.

His reluctance must have shown on his face, because she gave him a heart-melting look and said, "You ought to come. I wish you would."

How could anyone fight that look? It wasn't possible.

"Okay," he said, feeling like he'd just slipped off the edge of something. "I'll be there. I don't have to dress up or anything, do I?"

"No," she laughed. As her laugh gave way to a gentle smile, she said. "Good night, Gil."

"'Night Emily. Take care."

He walked back down the block, huffing against the cold he hadn't noticed earlier. He only got to the corner before he turned and stood, watching until the light finally went out in one of Emily's upstairs windows. He was freezing, standing there on the corner shivering like an idiot while he stared at some curtained window. On a house that looked like it walked out of a storybook, all white paint and gingerbread trim and cutesy window boxes. Four words banged around in his head.

She's getting to me.

Gil shrugged deeper into his coat and settled his hat farther down on his head, as if he could hide from it. *She's getting to me, Lord. Not that I didn't think it wouldn't happen eventually. But I didn't think it would be someone like her. She's so soft and tiny and lacy—we're nothing alike. I need someone who can shoulder their own. A strong partner. Someone not afraid of the dirt in my barn. In my life.*

She's not for me. And I'm sure not for her. I don't even like the way she smells.

That was an outright lie. If he knew it, surely God knew it. Truth was, he couldn't get the way she smelled out of his head. It was like a horror movie—something you were sure you hated but couldn't shake.

Gil, you jerk, you just decided she smells like a horror movie. How stupid is that? Now do you see why you don't belong anywhere near someone like her?

But he wanted to be near her. All the time.

He would have said yes to Character Day even if she told him he had to wear a tie.

Oh, man, he was in trouble.

"Ethan told me I'd find you here. He practically had to draw me a map. Your place is huge."

Emily was the last person Gil expected to see today. He was with Lady Macbeth in the clearing he called "the cathedral," a picturesque spot of tall pines and a sweeping view that often kept him sane on his worst days. The guys on the farm knew to look here if they couldn't find him anywhere else, but they also knew not to bug him if they found him here. It was never stated, but the cathedral was off-limits to almost everyone but Gil. It surprised him that Ethan had sent her up here. It hinted at things he didn't like Ethan thinking about.

"What brings you all the way out here?" he asked.

"I brought your gloves back. Wow, this spot is beautiful."

Gil put down the shears he was using to clear away some dead brush. "Fifteen miles out of your way for a pair of gloves? You could've just left them with Ethan at the house."

"Yes, I could have, but I seem to remember you being persnickety about the payment of debts. Besides, maybe I was just looking for an excuse to come visit Lady Macbeth."

He watched her walk around the edge of the clearing, taking in the view. The cathedral was a wondrous place. The tree trunks seemed to reach up into the clouds, gathering the streaming shafts of sunlight and sending them glittering on the snowy ground. The scent of pine sharpened the air, and the quiet was so powerful it settled deep into his chest.

"It's pretty," she said. "Ethan called it the cathedral. Is it a favorite spot of yours?"

"It's sort of a sacred spot for me. I come here when the farm is making me crazy and I need to get my soul back in order. Which means I come here a lot."

Lady Macbeth, always one to remember a fan, trotted over to give Emily a friendly nudge. "She thinks you've brought her treats. I've got one in my coat pocket if you want to give it to her."

Emily looked reluctant. Aha, so she wasn't really out here to cozy up to 'Beth. The knowledge buzzed inside him. "You said you were here to see her, so be neighborly and give the girl a cookie." He reached into his coat pocket and pulled out an oatmeal cookie. "Spread your hand out flat like a plate and put the cookie on it. She'll take it from you. Girl to girl with baked goods—you can't lose."

"I can't lose a finger? She won't bite?"

"'Beth knows when people mean her harm, and when people mean her good. She's smart that way. You can trust her."

"You're sure?" She looked unconvinced.

Gil walked over and stroked 'Beth's neck. "Horses are trustworthy by nature. Did somebody teach you not to trust a horse? You have a fall when you were young?"

"Not really. More like a bad experience. Not that there are lots of chances to have horse experiences in Ohio"

"You can fall off a horse in France and it'd still hurt."

"This is more like embarrassing." She fiddled with the gloves she was still holding. "It's nothing, really. 'Pony Ride Gone Wrong' is hardly a headline for tragedy. I didn't even get very hurt."

He knew instantly that wasn't true. Sometimes the regrettable, embarrassing stuff left the deepest scars of all. "Horses are big. Girls are little. That's a touchy combination sometimes." He deliberately softened his voice, but didn't move any closer to her. "What happened?"

"My seventh birthday party. I'd decided I wanted a princess theme, and I wanted pony rides on white ponies."

He grinned. "You do think in specifics, I'll give you that." Gil settled onto the bench he'd hewn out of logs that sat at one edge of the circle. She began wandering around the other edge, away from 'Beth. Of course, he knew if she kept pacing she'd eventually end up right next to her. And him. He stayed silent.

"I had this idea in my head about how elegant it would be to ride a white pony. I had the whole party planned out in my head, how I'd be the first to ride, how my friends would ride after me, what I'd wear—all the classic girl stuff. Of course, white ponies are a bit more challenging to find on the pony-ride circuit, and my parents had to go with a, shall we say, less reputable outfit. The man who hoisted me up onto that pony didn't look very princely, and he didn't pay a whole lot of attention to what was going on."

She had walked halfway around the circle now, and was only a few feet from his bench. She stopped pacing and hugged her jacket to her body, giving a little shrug as she looked at him. "Long story short, the horse spooked and took off with me on top of it, and…well…it didn't exactly go the way I hoped."

"That's a lousy thing to do to a girl on her birthday."

"I ended up with a bloody nose, a muddy dress and a much shorter birthday party than anyone planned. I mean, that bothered me and such, but it was more the part about being on something I couldn't control. Feeling like I couldn't stop that horse or anything it chose to do to me." Emily turned around and began retracing her steps around the circle. "Naturally I understand that it wasn't the horse's fault. Hundreds of safe docile pony rides occur every year, with attentive handlers who keep control of their animals. I know that. But the feeling of hanging on for dear life while that thing bolted around the park isn't one I've ever been able to shake."

Gil stared at her. No wonder she liked to have her details lined up and felt comfortable with her high level of control. That'd be a scary experience for any girl, much less one of Emily's cautious nature.

"It's silly, isn't it? To put a perfectly nice horse like 'Beth in the same category as that carnival pony?"

Gil got up and held out the cookie he'd been holding the whole time. "Silly? Not at all. Solvable? Completely. You're one cookie away from a new outlook on horses. Come on, let 'Beth redeem her kind." He handed her the cookie. "Spread your hand out, just like I showed you."

Emily opened her hand and put the cookie on her palm. Slowly, cautiously, she held her hand out in 'Beth's direction. 'Beth sniffed at the cookie, then used her big, rough lips to pick it up as delicately as any high-society lady selecting a tea sandwich. Emily erupted in tense laughter as 'Beth's not-so-ladylike whiskers tickled her bare palm.

"The trick to most animals—and most people, near as I can tell—is to treat 'em with respect. Even if you have to look hard to find something respectable about them." He walked over to the edge of the clearing and stared down at the rolling hillside.

"You respect your guys. Is that your secret?"

"I respect their abilities even if I think their choices…well…often their choices stink worse than my barn. At first."

"Do they respect you? In return?"

"Not always. Actually, never at first. At first it feels like I'm pouring attention down a black hole. They won't respond. When everybody tells you you're bad and worthless, you start to believe it. When you grow up in a world where the only way to get what you want is to take it, earning it seems like a waste of time. They try to put me off by bein' as bad as possible, testing to see if I really mean what I say." He turned back to face her. "That's when it's hard, and I end up here a lot, asking God for strength and endurance and the guts to do it all over again one more day."

"Does it ever get easier?"

"Ninety percent of the time, I get through to these guys quick enough. It's the other ten percent that takes it out of me. There's always one every year. One guy whose neck I want to wring, who I want to shake until he sees the chances he's throwing away. But then one guy turns, and the rest of them catch on and we make it to the finish line."

"The homestretch," she added.

"Not very inventive, but it keeps me focused."

She suddenly crossed her arms over her chest, frowning at him. "Gil Sorrent, you're a shameless fraud."

"What?" he said, startled by her strong words.

"You've got the world convinced you're a dark, hard man, someone to be feared, when in truth you're just a big softie handing out cookies when nobody's looking. I see what's hiding behind that well-placed scowl."

Without realizing it, she'd voiced the thought he'd been trying to ignore—she saw through his defenses. She was getting to him, all right, getting to him faster than he knew what to do with. There was a part of him that wanted to scoop her up right that moment, to put her on 'Beth with him and show her how a horse's gallop could be an exhilarating thing. To hold her tight to him and hear her whoop with joy as they barreled across the hillside, ducking in and out of the trees and tearing across the pastures. The urge almost took him over before he had to shake his head to come to his senses. That kind of thing couldn't happen. Not yet, maybe not ever.

"Cut that out," he said, trying to sound gruff but instead barely hiding his sudden surge of emotion. "You'll ruin my reputation."

Chapter Seventeen

Character Day was exactly what Gil expected: an hour of sitting in a hard folding chair in a stuffy high-school auditorium watching students amble up to the stage to accept sheets of paper. The quote—evidently every Character Day had a theme quote—made him more uncomfortable than his metal chair. It was the one by Edmund Burke: "The only thing necessary for evil to triumph is for good men to do nothing."

He sat in the back, near the door. Even though he'd promised Emily he would come, he felt as though he didn't belong here. Character Day was all about upstanding citizens and virtue—not exactly his home turf. The guys had given him grief earlier when he'd showed up at lunch in what Ethan jokingly called his "dress pants"—a pair of khakis rather than the ubiquitous blue jeans that were his daily wardrobe. When Ethan pulled out of him where he was going, and that Emily was the speaker, the jokes didn't let up for a full ten minutes. But Mac, he was the worst of all. When Mac found out, he went into a four minute tirade listing all the times and places he'd seen Gil and Emily together and teasing him with an assortment of highly annoying speculations.

It took him a moment to find Emily among all the faculty onstage. She sat off to one side, her feet tucked underneath her as tightly as they had been in his office that day. She wore a darker color dress than normal and she'd pinned her hair up, but she had a signature-color pastel silk scarf around her neck. Gil felt almost like he was looking at a reflection of Emily—some darker, one-dimensional copy of the real person. Something told him she must have looked like that on the day of Ash's funeral. The sensation that thought produced in his gut was not a pleasant one.

Howard made a long, mayoral introduction, comprised of a short bio of Emily sandwiched between two monologues on Middleburgian pride. Only Howard, Gil thought to himself, could introduce someone else and *still* make it all about him. Sandy should have made the introduction, but wrestling the microphone out of Howard's hands at public events like this was beyond even Sandy's negotiating skills.

"I suppose you're wondering why I'm up here," Emily said, her voice a bit shaky as she took the podium and went through the noisy process of bending the microphone down to her height. They'd had to move a box behind the podium so that she could be easily seen, and it had made for an awkward transition after her introduction. "If I were you, I'd have thought some well-known do-gooder would be up here talking today. Most of you know me from a few years ago when my husband's death made the papers a lot. Ash Montague was a good man—a great man, actually, and he would have been the kind of guy to stand up here and be inspirational. He believed in doing good. He believed in finding the role God had set up for you in the world and going at it with all you had. God gave him an amazing musical talent and a mind for mechanics, and he figured out how to make use of those gifts and build himself a career. Now most of you wouldn't think of a piano tuner as an heroic guy, but if any of you had Ash coach your Little League team or teach your Sunday School class, you know a little bit about what made him a hero to me."

A few murmurs went through the crowd. Gil suspected it was those whom Ash had taught or coached agreeing with what Emily had said.

"I'm gonna surprise you today, though, by not talking about Ash. I'm gonna talk about another man who changed my life forever. A man I imagine most of you don't even know existed." She went on to briefly describe the night of the murder.

And the man who could have stopped it.

"We know from several sources that he was close enough to have stepped in. Ash told the police as he lay—" her voice cracked and Gil felt his heart crack with it "—lay…dying…that he'd asked the man to help. Begged him. To step in and stop a terrible crime. To do something instead of standing back and being horrified."

The room fell silent. Sandy was right—this would be a speech these students wouldn't soon forget. The image of her standing there, trying to hold it together long enough to let these kids see the consequences of inaction, the cost of apathy, was indelible. The students would never forget it because the truth is that powerful.

Gil would never forget it because it was the exact moment his heart broke. Snapped. It was the clean, sharp end of something that hadn't even really begun.

She went on about the pain of never finding that witness, of knowing her husband had been left to die. Gil had never wanted to leave a place so badly in all his life.

"That man's crime was greater to me than Ash's murder, because he was one of us. I cannot think of Ash's murderer as an ordinary man—he had some hideous motive, some all-consuming greed that made him an awful man. Most of us are not awful people. And yet, to me, the worse man is the one who is not brave enough to stop a crime, not the one who is awful enough to commit it. Not every crime is a choice—although I think many are—but every time you don't act, it *is* a choice. Your choice. Every one of you will have a chance—big or small—to choose whether or not to help out in a bad situation. I hope you remember today when that decision comes to you. Because to me, and, I think, to Ash, that's true character."

Gil sat there, his heart tearing open. It wasn't pity he felt—he knew the last thing she wanted was pity. It was a deep, crushing sorrow.

Sorrow because he was that worse kind of man.

The technical term for it was *accessory to murder,* but Gil had always found that phrase lacking. There wasn't a word for the lamentable act of holding down a human being while another man ended his life. For watching a murder and not stopping it. He'd done everything but hold the knife, and he'd been just as deaf to the victim's pleas for mercy as the man Emily condemned.

Accessory to murder. He'd done something so close to—no, not even close to, *worse than*—the act she deplored that he knew she could never love him. They were so different that it had been almost impossible before.

It was beyond impossible now.

Gil could only take in bits and pieces of the rest of her speech. He dimly registered her call to the students to be people who stepped in. To do the hard, right thing and get involved rather than stand by and watch life hurt the weak or take a good man down. She didn't sound bitter or spiteful, but her bone-deep contempt for "the man who would not save my husband" weighted her words.

A weight that crushed him as he sat in that miserable folding chair.

Finally, when he thought he couldn't even breathe anymore, she ended her speech and the room rose to its feet. Sandy rushed to the podium and wrapped Emily in a big hug, embracing her until the two of them were wiping tears from their eyes.

He slipped from the room in a haze of pain and regret. His only thought was that he'd have to admit his cowardice to her, and he didn't think he could survive the confession.

Gil was so intent on groping his way through the fog in his brain, just trying to find his truck and get home, that he nearly knocked over the policeman in his path.

"Sorrent?"

Gil shook himself and tried to focus on the man in front of him. "Huh?"

"Gil Sorrent, right? I'm glad I found you—I've been calling the farm for the last twenty minutes."

"What's up?"

"We picked up one of your guys in town, Mr. Sorrent. A Mark Santini. You're familiar with the name?"

What was Mark doing in town? The guys weren't due in town today; Ethan was having them clear brush from the south pasture. "I am. Is he okay?"

"Well, I don't know how much detail I can give you, but

we caught him breaking and entering. He was cleaning out the cash register of a local business when someone saw him through the shop window and called it in."

No, Lord, no. Not now. Gil wiped his hands down his face and tried to think of the right course of action. "I'll give you whatever you need. Full cooperation." He looked up at the officer. "Are...are you sure? Which business?"

"A bath shop called West of Paris. Evidently the owner's inside, she was part of some assembly today. He must have known she'd be away from the store."

"Emily Montague," Gil said, his voice gruff.

"Yeah, that's her. So you know her?"

If God asked for volunteers to lie down and die at that moment, Gil would have gladly stepped forward. "Yes, I know her."

The officer pointed toward the door Gil had just come through. "Well, seeing as I need the both of you, you'd best come point her out to me so I can get you both into town on the double."

She'd done it.

Emily had given the speech. It was a tremendous relief, and it felt like a giant step forward. It had been hard to bring all the pain back up—and then again, it hadn't, because the pain had never really left. She'd found ways to ignore it, gloss over it or deny it, but it hadn't ever truly healed. She'd spent most of that first year scanning strangers' faces, as if she'd know the bystander by some look in his eyes. They'd had tiny clues, and there'd been a police search, but no one ever really thought they'd find the man who was there that night.

She wasn't healed. Not by a long shot. But today felt

like a step closer to it. It was that, as much as relief, that brought the tears to her eyes when Sandy hugged her. *That's what good friends do,* she thought. *They nudge you up to the hard places where you need to go. Thank you, Lord, for friends like Sandy.*

There were all kinds of congratulations from teachers, students and even from Peter Epson, who'd volunteered to cover the event for the paper. "This is a great story," he told her as he shook her hand. "You did a super job up there."

Emily smiled. "Thanks, Peter. It was an important thing to do."

"Emily?"

She turned, glad to hear Gil's voice. She'd wanted to know what he thought of the speech. From the looks of things, he hadn't liked it at all—the man looked absolutely dismal.

"Gil, you *did* come." She went to shake his hand, but his bristling demeanor stopped her.

"Emily, this is Officer Ryan. You need to come to the shop right away."

The circumstance of being summoned by a grim-looking police officer shot through Emily like lightning. An old, deep-seeded panic erupted out of nowhere. "What's wrong?"

"There's been a robbery at your business, Ms. Montague."

"A robbery?" Emily said, not caring that it was a little too loudly. "At the shop?"

Gil took her by one elbow and began guiding her toward the door. "Mark broke into your cash register while he knew you'd be here," he said tightly. "Someone saw him and called the police."

Emily spun out of his grasp. "Mark? From Home-stretch? One of *your guys* robbed my store?" She took a step back from him, feeling like someone had just knocked the wind out of her. "Mark robbed me?"

Emily felt the panic growing with surprising speed as she made her way back to the store. Gil insisted on driving her, and while being with him felt uncomfortable given the circumstances, she knew she didn't have enough wits about her to drive well. She found she didn't have enough wits even to offer a decent resistance when he insisted. Instead, she let him guide her into the truck and take her downtown, but neither of them spoke on the trip.

Pulling up to West of Paris was a shock to her system. The flurry of men in dark blue and the barrage of questions took her back almost instantly to the horrible time after Ash's death. It didn't make much sense—a minor break-in shouldn't have felt anywhere near as traumatic as the murder of a spouse—but this didn't seem to be about logic. Old feelings and fears came back with a vengeance, offering no perspective or guidance. The policeman asking her about locks and keys frightened her just as much as the one who had asked her what type of keychain Ash carried.

Things were strewn everywhere. Linens were tossed about like dirty laundry, and several vases and soap dishes lay shattered on the floor. One table by the front window was knocked over, and policemen were taking photographs. The pop of camera flashes screamed "crime scene."

Emily had just gotten to the place in life where she didn't think of herself as a victim. And now, she was one again. It felt like the world's evil was reaching up to pull her back into the pit she'd spent years escaping. The horrible old sensations—the tangled thoughts, the thud of her pulse in her ears, the feeling that the room didn't hold enough oxygen—came roaring back with the sound of glass crunching underfoot.

Worst of all was the cash register. Once a lovely old lady, elegant and classic, the antique register lay battered on the floor like a wrecked car. The drawer had been yanked out, its handle now misshapen as if someone had taken a crowbar to it. A few coins and a handful of receipts lay strewn about the dented remains. Emily reached down and picked up the marble Tommy Lee Lockwood had given her, feeling it like a physical blow to her stomach. She'd not yet gone to the bank—all her sales income from Valentine's Day had still been in the register.

Had been. Now, it was all gone.

It was worse than some random act. This had been deliberate and calculated. Mark had set out to get her and succeeded. Had chosen the exact moment he knew she'd be elsewhere and robbed her in broad daylight. In some ways, that made it even worse than Ash's murder—Ash had been in the wrong place at the wrong time, but this felt alarmingly personal. It made her ill to think of it.

Gil seemed to sense enough of her distress to keep a distance, but he wouldn't leave. She was dimly aware of his presence as she stumbled through the shop, touching a shard of glass or folding a tea towel. Some part of her knew he was as angered by this as she, that he wasn't responsible for what had happened. Another part of her blindly blamed all of Homestretch Farm for bringing crime to her doorstep.

Janet Bishop, owner of the hardware store down the street, came over personally to see to the replacement of the glass panes and locks in her back door. With a host of men firing questions at her, she welcomed a woman's compassion.

"It's terrible," Janet said, wrapping Emily in a great big hug. "You, of all people. You just sit tight, and we'll have you fixed up in no time. That pane will be replaced within the hour. I brought you three types of new locks to choose from, okay?" Janet seemed to understand Emily's need to do something concrete in all this confusion, something to help her regain control. She put three boxes down in front of her, opening the tops to display three shiny sets of brass fixtures. "All of them will do the job better than that old lock. Top-notch, each of them. You just decide the one you want." They were all elegant, graceful lock sets. It was comforting, in an odd way. Somehow she'd been sure Janet was going to bring big, ugly, institutional-looking things that Emily felt would scream "you're not safe anymore" every time she used them.

She decided on one with filigree around the deadbolt, thankful that Janet understood why choosing stronger new locks might be such an emotional decision. She'd never been more grateful for her friendship with Janet than she was this afternoon. Janet handled the glass replacement with the same comforting sensitivity.

Gil stayed at the shop for a while, inspecting the new locks, sweeping things up, keeping his anger down to a low simmer. She knew he was putting off his visit to the police station—who knows what he would do when he finally got a chance to talk to Mark? Even while he was keeping things under control, he looked like he wanted to kick something hard and far.

The whole town had waited for Homestretch to bring crime to Middleburg. People had lived in distrust the first year—herself included—and while no one would openly admit it, everyone had been surprised when there hadn't been a single incident. Everyone had waited for a problem that never arrived.

Until now. Now those unspoken fears had come to fruition, and Emily was keenly aware that her misfortune might likely spell the end of Homestretch Farm. The rational part of her felt bad, but the irrational, wounded part of her wanted someone else to pay for what had happened. For the sense of safe, small-town peace that was now gone.

Chapter Eighteen

Gil stood up against the massive mantel that capped his living-room fireplace. It was a large, rustic room, lined with solid beams and wood paneling that had seen decades of history. This was the room where all of Homestretch's most important events took place—good and bad. Today felt squarely in the latter.

He looked at his Bible, sitting in its customary place on the corner of that mantel, and said a prayer for the right words. The farm knew Mark had gone missing, but only Gil and Ethan knew the extent of the troubles now facing Homestretch. And no one knew yet if Mark had acted alone.

"What's up, sir?" Larry asked.

The use of pleasantries like *sir, ma'am, please,* and *thank you* was one of the first lessons at Homestretch Farm. When the newbies came, they mostly just grunted at each other and everyone else, using such a complicated form of slang that Gil often had to ask for a translation. Gil made it clear that he didn't expect to be called *sir* in casual conversation; only in more formal situations like house meetings or in public. The boys were instructed to use *sir* and *ma'am* at all times in town, and so far only Steve had been recalcitrant in doing so. Then again, Steve bucked the system on everything.

This kind of stuff was always tricky. Accuse them of consorting with Mark, and they'd clam right up in defiance. Come down too soft, and they'd think only Mark got caught and not fess up when it would do the most good. They'd look for the easy out, the clean getaway, because that's the life they'd had. The concept of the "hard but right thing" never came easily to these guys. Most of them hadn't ever had Character Day, or role models, or even parents who paid them any kind of attention.

"Homestretch has a big problem, and we're going to put our heads together and figure out what to do about it." He waited, still facing the fire, for one of them to give the What'd-we-do-now? speech. "Everybody always blames us," was a favorite defense of these guys, mostly because it worked. Playing victim of the system was a tried-and-true defense in their world. It deflected blame and evoked pity—a few favorite tools of the outcast and rebellious. He'd heard more versions of it than he could count. Most of them he'd used once or twice himself.

No response came. Well, now, perhaps he should take that as a good sign. He tucked his hands in his pants pockets and turned slowly, leaning back against the mantel. The glow of the flames played across the faces looking back at him, and Gil was startled at the strength of emotion welling up inside. The guys each had a different expression, from defiant to annoyed to hurt. This group had driven him crazy with more grief and more headaches than he cared to recount. They'd also given him more satisfaction than any year he could remember.

A couple of them had finally come to care what he thought about them, and that was huge. These guys had spent so many years learning how not to care, that once you got them to care the floodgates opened up. That's why the horses made such great therapists—they were safe places to learn to care for something. Eventually, caring for something could teach them to care for someone, and that was the beginning of everything.

Would it all be over now?

Gil pushed that thought away. He couldn't afford to dwell on that problem right now. His immediate task was to find Mark's accomplice—if he had one—and set him straight. Damage control. Let the guys know the extent of the threat Mark had brought down on the farm without giving them reason to panic and throw in the towel.

Even though he felt that way himself.

Gil started with the facts. "Ms. Montague's bath shop was broken into." Passive statement of fact. No accusations, not even use of a suspicious pronoun like *somebody*.

Gil could usually count on Marty to start things off, so it wasn't a surprise when Marty leaned forward and snarled, "You think we did it." Larry kicked Marty's foot with his own, at which point Marty revised his question to a biting, "You think we did it, *sir*."

"No, we already know who did it. But yes, you all were immediately suspect." The defensive moans started up, and Gil silenced them with a raised hand. "That should come as no surprise if you stop and think about it, so don't get all riled up just yet. Y'all made no secret of your wanting that soap of hers. I even know one of you managed to convince Peter Epson he'd get a girl with it."

"Well," Steven boasted, his secret out, "he was such an easy mark. Totally gullible."

"You and all your machismo just too much to deny, hmm?" Paulo cut in.

"That, gentlemen," Gil interrupted, determined to keep the focus where it belonged, "is a conversation for another day. We got enough trouble today as it is—no need to borrow more."

Gil leaned one elbow up on the mantelpiece, trying to calm his body language despite his rising temper. "Someone from Homestretch knocked off West of Paris. *After* Ms. Montague was so nice to you. Mighty lousy, if you ask me."

"Who's askin' you?" said Marty, leaning back in the huge leather chair. He crossed his arms over his chest defensively.

"I just spent the last hour bein' asked all kinds of things by the Middleburg Police Department," Gil shot back.

"And we know, *sir,* that you don't take to the idea of anybody messin' with Miss Montague," said Paulo, who always thought everything was about women anyway.

"Yeah," said Marty with the tone of someone about to say something dangerous. Larry kicked him again, harder this time. "Sir," Marty added almost under his breath. Then, as if it had just dawned on the him, Marty added, "Mark's not here."

"No, Mark's not here." Gil gave the guys a moment for that to sink in. He wasn't sure who'd already realized Mark wasn't in the room and kept quiet about it, or who actually hadn't caught on to his absence. "That's because Mark's in jail. Under arrest. He figured out Emily would be at the high school giving her speech—her speech on why it's important to do the right thing—and took that opportunity to pay a little social call to her cash register."

Grumbles ran through the guys. Gil noted most of them had what he considered to be genuine looks of surprise or anger. Again, he chose to take that as a good sign.

"That idiot," Larry finally said, and the group chimed in with a host of less-polite names for Mark. "I'm glad he got caught. At least everyone'll know it wasn't us that did it."

"Don't be stupid," Steven said. "That won't stop them. They'll think we were all in on it. People around here are just waiting for us to screw up. Thinkin' we're nobodies who don't belong here. You see the looks. Mark just handed 'em more reasons to run us outta here."

A smattering of "yep"s and "uh-huh"s backed Steven up.

"So now you know why I need to ask this, and why I'm only gonna ask once: Did any of you know anything about this?" He stared each guy down, one at a time, and got a "no" from each of them.

He believed them. Not that it made him feel any better.

Friday morning, Mac stared incredulously at Gil from the passenger seat of the truck. "You can't. You can't seriously be thinking of shutting Homestretch down."

Gil knew Mac would try and talk him out of it, but he was so wound up he needed to bounce the idea off someone. He was furious with Ethan for letting Mark sneak out on his watch, and talking with Emily was definitely out of the question, so he'd called Mac. "I own it, I can do whatever I want with it. I give these guys everything. I put my gut into this every single day. And I ain't never, ever regretted it like I do right now. I'd rather beat the town council to the punch then let them take me down." He punched in the farm gate security code and waited for the gate to slide open so they could head down to the police station.

"If you're so set, you mind telling me why I'm here?"

"Because I could use a cool head with me. And having to drive you back here to pick up your car is the only thing that's gonna stop me from pulling out onto I-75 and never looking back."

"Nice to be useful," Mac quipped. "You don't really mean that. You're not gonna close Homestretch. If you were, I'd be out on the side of the road by now." Mac scratched his chin and turned to look at Gil. "Come on, you can't tell me you didn't see this coming, sometime. It was bound to happen sooner or later. You can't expect to have a perfect record with this kind of guys."

"I can expect whatever I want."

"Well, yeah, but you're smarter than that. Actually, I'd be the first one to run you outta town if I thought that was the real trouble."

Gil shot him a look. "Would you?"

"You know why? Cuz it's only half of what's eating you—and don't try and tell me it ain't."

Gil refused to reply.

"They ran Emily's speech in the paper. I didn't have to read the whole thing to figure out what set you off. I don't think you're readin' this one right, Gil. You're making this about you when it ain't. I know how you think. She wasn't talking about you. If I know you, she doesn't even *know* about your record. So how can you put that on her till you tell her?"

"It's crystal clear what she'll think." Gil took a turn a little sharper than was necessary.

Mac pointed at him. "You've done it again. You've

decided what she thinks and how she'll act. You laid it all out in your head, down to the painful end, so rather than go through it, you'll just finish it off for the both of you before anyone has a chance. That way you stay in control."

"Cut it out, Mac." Gil put his sunglasses on even though it wasn't that bright out, and decided it had been a huge mistake to bring Mac along. It's not like he *needed* an escort to go fill out more paperwork at the police station and talk to Mark.

"You know, normally I would," Mac said, sitting back in his seat. "It's not like you're the sunniest guy to be around, even on a good day. Only a fool'd pick a fight with you on purpose."

"Kind of you to say so."

"But what you can't see is that you actually have a shot at bein' happy. That fluffy little gal finally got through to you—though I imagine even God's scratchin' His head on how she did it. So now, rather than get hurt, you're just gonna walk away because it got prickly. Like shutting down the farm. I have to say, I thought you had more guts than that, Gil. It's not like you to take the easy way out."

Gil pulled into a parking space in front of the police station and got out of the car. "You think this is easy? You see me enjoying myself anywhere here? Do I seem all sunny to you *now?*" He slammed the truck door shut and glared at Mac.

"Talk to her." Mac glared right back over the hood. "Nobody said you have to be a hero to get the girl, but you gotta tell her if you're gonna have a shot at it."

"There's no 'it' to have, Mac. There never was. I was just kidding myself."

Mac came around the truck and stood in front of Gil,

blocking his path. "Gil Sorrent, I've had your back for a long time, and I'm here to tell you there is. And you're a fool if you let it go without tryin'. A stupid, stubborn, lonely fool."

"I ain't no fool," Gil growled at him, checking the urge to deck his longtime friend.

"Maybe not, but you're five kinds of lonely and nobody wants you to stay that way. Least of all me." Mac threw his hands in the air. "I'll find my own ride home. Y'all go right on digging your big old lonely pit and crawl into it. I've said my piece. I'm done." With that, Mac stalked off down the street, oblivious to the fact that he'd still have to find his way back to Homestretch to get his car.

It was one thing to feel lonely. Another to admit it to yourself. But to have someone else *tell* you you're lonely—call you on it—that was worse yet. Nobody got to declare Gil's life lonely except him. Bein' thought of as lonely? That was about as low as you could get. Old men and softies got thought of as lonely.

Gil didn't mind not being liked. He didn't mind being thought of as mean, or gruff, or even a loner. But lonely? That was different. Lonely meant something else—Gil wasn't sure what that was, but he knew it felt weak. Vulnerable. Things he didn't like one bit. And right now he didn't like Mac one bit, either.

Even if he might be right. Which was the worst thing to consider of all.

Chapter Nineteen

Gil prowled into the police station ready to shred Mark alive. Mac had been supposed to calm him down, not goad him into a worse mood. It wasn't helping things that he got some I-told-you-so looks from officers as he filled out the miles of paperwork ending Mark's probational residency at Homestretch Farm.

He'd had high hopes for Mark. Mark was a challenge, a stiff-necked rebel, but he was smart and had a will that would have let him beat any odds. He was just training all his talents in the wrong direction. It stuck in Gil's craw that he couldn't turn that around. Instead, he'd handed Mark enough rope to go out and hang himself.

"You wanna see him?" the captain asked, initialing the last of a dozen forms as Gil handed them off.

Now there was a question. Sure, Gil wanted to do a dozen things to Mark—punch, shake, scold, knock upside the head—but see him? Did he really have anything to say to the guy? After a moment's thought, he decided that even if the only thing Mark took away from the visit was the look of supreme disappointment in Gil's eyes, maybe that would stick with him.

Middleburg's idea of a jail looked more like a walk-in closet with a barred door. Mark sat on a metal chair, tilted back on one wall with his feet propped up against the other. He had a cloying expression of accomplishment his face. Like he'd achieved his goal of hurting as many people as possible with a single act.

Gil almost walked out right then, too disgusted to attempt a conversation, but Mark turned at the sound of Gil's entrance and looked him in the eye. A cold, remorseless glare.

"You blew it," Gil said. "Happy?"

"Surprised?" Mark looked back at his sneakers. Sneakers Gil had bought him.

"I had better things in mind for you."

That brought a derisive snort from Mark. "You gonna say somethin' 'bout my potential? Spare me."

I tried to, Gil thought. *But you're gonna hit bottom, anyway. And it's a long, long way down.* "Brace yourself, Mark, it's gonna get really ugly from here on out."

"Uglier than the backsides of those horses? Than what you made me shovel every day?" He picked a splinter of wood off the knee of his jeans and threw it on the ground in front of the bars. Wood from Emily's door.

"Miles uglier. You're on your own, kid. I'm done with you."

Mark turned to him with fierce eyes. "Don't call me 'kid.'"

"You want to be called a man now?" Gil's anger boiled up beyond his restraint. "You hurt enough people now? Made enough of a mess of your life? You think that's how you earn it? You're nothing but a smart-mouthed punk of a—"

"I think we're done here," the captain said—clamping

a hand onto Gil's shoulder, pulling him away. "Let's everybody go home and cool off a bit."

As he pulled out of the police station, Gil thought a year in Iceland wouldn't be enough to cool him off.

Just when Gil thought his day couldn't get worse, there was a powder-blue VW bug parked outside the Homestretch gate when he drove up. Gil pulled his truck up next to the car, and Emily got out as he shut his engine off.

It wasn't a cold day for February, but she hugged herself as if she were freezing. "Why'd you send me a check, Gil?"

He'd found out the cost of the lock and door-window repairs, and sent her a check to cover the expense. "I believe in paying my debts. I thought that ought to cover the damages."

"You did nothing to my shop. Besides, I have insurance for that sort of thing. Mark is an adult. Why is his crime your responsibility?"

Gil leaned back against his truck. "I should think that'd be obvious. It's my job to keep these guys in-line."

She pulled the check out of her handbag and held it out to him. "Really? I thought it was your *ministry* to give these guys a second chance. One of them blew his chance. I don't see how that's your fault."

"You'll be alone in that opinion. It'll surely be seen as my fault. I'm the guy who brought them here, who put Middleburg at risk with all these 'seedy characters.'"

"This isn't about you."

"Isn't it? You've no idea the defense I run for these guys. The comments I fend off. The stares I ignore. Lots of folks are more than ready to write them off. Women who clutch their purses tighter when they walk by. And now? Now they'll all be right. Look at all you've lost—look at what Mark did to you. People love your shop, they know you, and this is all they need to shut down Homestretch Farm. When's the last time we had a break-in in Middleburg? Years. How can I argue with that when someone calls— because you know someone will—to shut down the farm?"

"That won't happen," she defended.

"How can you say that?" he snapped back. "You should be leading the fight. You were nice to them and look how Mark repaid you!"

"I'm not saying I'm not upset, but the door's repaired, the lock's replaced, and they've recovered the money. I've got justice. I don't need vengeance on top of it. I'm not going to call for you to shut down the farm."

"Maybe you should. I'm sure thinking about it."

"Gil, even if every one of these guys bashed in my lock and stole my money, it doesn't erase all the other men you've helped. All the 'gut,' as you say, that you've poured into other men. I look at them now, and I don't see hoodlums. And that's *your* doing. *You* did that. Mark doesn't get to erase that. I won't let him."

Why did she have to be so upstanding? Her compassion made it all so much worse. "Will you *stop* trying to save this, Emily?"

She looked at him, stunned. "Why?" It would be hard to put more pain into that one word.

"Because some things can't be saved. Or shouldn't."

She blew out a breath. "You're the last person on earth who should say that. How can you think that when most people wouldn't give those guys half the chances you give them?" She narrowed her eyes at him. "What's wrong?"

"You've just had your store broken into and you need

to ask what's *wrong?*" He'd thought the robbery had done it for him—broken it off so he wouldn't have to. But no. He was going to have to spell it out for her, let her see exactly who she was dealing with here. In his mind he could already see the expression that would come over her face. That subtle, suspicious shift when someone stops seeing you as human and consigns you to something just above a beast. He had to tell her. But here? Now? Outside his gate, along the side of the road like some kind of accident? It was the worst possible place. Then again, is there a perfect place to end a relationship? A choice spot to break somebody's heart?

Do it now. At least then it'll all be over. "I'm not some kind of hero," Gil began. How do you explain rock bottom to someone like Emily? She was someone whose life had been scarred, but she'd never sent herself there of her own free will. How could he ever, even for a moment, forget that she was a crime victim? That he was a criminal?

Gil pulled the words from somewhere deep in his chest, and they felt as though they were ripping their way out of him as he spoke. "I told you I went to jail. But I didn't tell you *why* I went to jail. I kid myself that it doesn't matter. But it matters a whole lot. You asked me once why I try to turn these guys around."

"I remember," she said, a bit of alarm creeping into her voice.

"You want to know the real reason why? I do it because nobody turned me around. At least not fast enough. Not in time. One night I found myself holding a bloody man on a street curb. But I wasn't holding him up. I was holding him *down*. Down, Emily. Pinning him so my buddy could hurt him. And you know what? It was so easy to do—to go along with it. I didn't try to stop him or put up so much as a bit of resistance. No, as a matter of fact, I wanted to be him. To be strong and bad enough to kill someone. You'd be amazed how far you can fall before you figure out you've gone all the way down."

Gil turned and planted his palms on the hood of his truck so he wouldn't have to look at her. "That's the kind of guy I was. I didn't care what I did or who I hurt. I looked up to guys who killed or shot, admired how tough they were. I *helped*. I held the guy down while my buddy knifed him. You said it yourself, Emily, that's the worst kind of man. Not strong enough to commit a crime, but not brave enough to stop one."

"You…weren't there the night they killed Ash. That wasn't you." Her voice sounded a million miles away. She said it as though she needed him to confirm it.

"No, but I could have been, so what's the difference? One's as bad as the other. We don't belong together. Now you know why."

"The man in front of me couldn't have done that." She sounded as if she were trying to reconcile things in her head. To make sense of something he already knew would never make sense, especially not to her.

"Yeah, well, I clean up pretty good, don't I? But that kind of slate won't wipe clean, Emily. Don't even try."

He could hear her pacing a few steps behind him. "I…I don't know what in the world to make of this." The footsteps stopped, and he knew she was right behind him. "How could you keep this from me? Until now?"

"Because I'm a coward, Emily. You need me to spell it out for you any further?"

An unbelievably long silence hung in the air. He

couldn't bring himself to turn and look at her. He couldn't look her in the eye—not now, probably not ever. He'd thought he'd known how bad it would hurt, but he was wrong. It hurt so much worse.

"You don't even see it, do you?" she said softly.

"See what? What is there to see?"

"You're acting just like they do, showing me how bad you are so I'll go away. You've saved up the one thing sure to ruin us, sure to send me running. And you bring it out now. I got too close, didn't I?"

He made the mistake of turning to argue with her. The hard edge in her eyes—those soft, warm eyes that had done him in—stunned him to silence.

"Well, congratulations," she went on, her voice rising. "You're really bad. You're worse than I thought. It's really awful." She began pacing again, gesturing wildly with her hands. "So what happens now? Does the Earth open up and swallow you whole? Do I run off screaming? Is that why you did this on the side of the road? To make sure I ran?"

Why was she dragging it out like this? "You and I—we can't work—don't you get that?" Gil bellowed in frustration. "None of this goes away, ever. It's not like I just need a good confession to be a better man."

They stood there, in the cold at the side of the road, for an excruciating length of time. He wanted to tell her to go away but he couldn't make the words come out.

"I'm not gonna say it's okay." She leaned against her car, looking drained. "I don't know what it is. I don't know what to do."

"There isn't really anything to do, is there?" Gil felt like someone had taken a sledgehammer to his chest. Another gaping silence. He kept his eyes on the gravel by the side of the road, dying to get out of there, helpless to leave.

"How old were you? When it happened."

Come on, Lord, have mercy, make her stop. I'm dying here. "Old enough to know better."

"How old, Gil?" She was fighting tears.

"Sixteen." Like that made any difference.

Twice she took a breath as if to say something, but never did. Then, without even so much as looking at him, she got into her car and left.

Gil punched the fender of his truck hard enough to bruise his hand. He picked up a stone that had fallen off the gatepost and threw it so hard it sailed yards into the pasture on the other side of the road.

He'd thought his heart had already broken, that the quick, sharp snap back in the high-school auditorium was the final blow.

The long, slow crush he felt as he pulled the truck up the drive was infinitely worse.

Chapter Twenty

Even though she felt like normal life was beyond her grasp, Emily flipped the sign to Open Saturday morning and pulled up the shades at West of Paris. How on earth was she supposed to function today? How does anyone play helpful shopkeeper when her heart's been twisted into knots?

The new locks were actually rather pretty—Janet had done a fine job. A brass plate around the knobs even hid the spot where Mark had tried to pry open the door. The table with the broken leg was splinted with some duct tape and paint stirrers Janet had brought over and covered with a tablecloth that ran to the floor so no one could tell.

But Emily knew.

The linens were all neatly back in their stacks, and the scratches in the floor from the broken glass were almost impossible to see. Short of the missing cash register, any casual customer would probably have no idea anything was wrong.

Tidying up West of Paris was the easy fix.

Emily had absolutely no idea what to do about Gil. How to face him. She'd thought she had prepared herself for whatever dark patches his past held. But she hadn't been at all prepared for something so personally painful. She was supposed to be getting past that. She'd just given a speech that was supposed to *prove* she was getting past that. Past the years of detesting whoever it was that had stood by and watched Ash die. Now, it was as though it had all happened yesterday—the wounds reopened instantly.

She'd been a wreck when she came back from the farm. Her emotions warred within her all night. She barely slept. Despite her horror at his admission, the depth of her feelings for him hadn't disappeared. She couldn't understand how those feelings could exist along with the shock at his crime. When he'd said "accessory to felony," she'd never thought it could mean "accessory to murder." Somehow, her brain wouldn't allow her even to consider the possibility.

It all seemed too impossibly cruel.

She sorted distractedly through a delivery of greeting cards, trying to do something productive. What was this tangle of feelings? There was wonder, she thought as she put the children's birthday cards into their assigned slots on the display. Her heart had reopened itself to wondrously new yet surprisingly familiar feelings. There was sadness—mourning, even, for lost innocence—which was silly, for who comes into love innocent at her age? Who doesn't bring the past's wounds into a second love?

Emily removed the leftover Valentine's Day cards from the display. Did she love Gil? *Could* she love Gil, knowing what she knew now? Could she ever think of him as different from the bystander at Ash's murder? Nothing she felt made any sense—she only knew she felt off-kilter and confused.

There was a sliver of thankfulness, she thought as she placed the thank-you cards in their spaces. Part of her believed she'd never feel for any man again. She had convinced herself that what she had with Ash was a once-in-a-lifetime thing.

The cards that captured her mood, sadly enough, were the get-well-soon ones. She did feel ill. Wounded, broken and unwell. But this didn't feel as if it was going to get well anytime soon.

What have You sent me, Father? I thought my heart had died along with Ash, and You give it to a damaged man who risks his money and reputation on criminals? Someone with a past so hurtful to me? I can't live with that. Surely You know I'd want anything but this. How could You bring that speech into my life and then do this? Fool me into believing I could finally forgive and then show me how I can't? I can't trust Your plan for my life when You do this to me.

The truth of that thought cut her so sharply she sank to the floor amid the boxes and wrapping. *I've never trusted Your plan for my life, have I? Not since Ash. I pretend to have faith, but only as long as it's comfortable.*

Why?

The answer was awful. *Because I think Your plan for me failed.*

O Lord, it's true: I think You failed me. People of faith can't really believe that, can they? Emily leaned back against the counter and stared into space, stunned by the discovery of her own mistrust. Looking back on the years since the murder, though, Emily could clearly see she'd rarely trusted God at all. She'd never let Him guide her, only presented Him with requests. Submitted her solutions for approval. What did she do every morning? Hand God a to-do list in the guise of praying over it. Tell Him what she wanted. Had she ever once even asked Him what His plan was for her life? Listened instead of petitioned?

Never.

"I've spent my whole life telling You what to do," she whispered to the air, as if she needed to hear it aloud to grasp the enormity of it.

Was it so surprising that God brought her to a place where she had no idea what to do next? Where no option made sense? Where she didn't have one of her famous solutions?

To a place where she had no choice but to hush and listen?

There, on the floor, Emily Montague sought God.

For real. Maybe for the first time in her life.

My life is Yours. It's always been Yours, but I snatched it back when Ash died. And I've made a mess of it.

These sins felt too large for her own faith, too huge for the theology she had. Truth didn't feel like truth anymore. She felt as though she'd just stared down the limits of her faith and found herself beyond what she could handle. Here, now, she could barely be sure she had the faith to hope things would sort themselves out.

I've never really laid it all at Your feet, have I? I've never, not once, prayed "Thy will be done." So I'll start now. This whole mess—all I am, all I've done, all I'm up against—it's all Yours. All Gil is, all he's done, all he means to me—they're all Yours, too. Have Your will in this. Teach me to listen. I'm not sure I know how.

"Thy will be done." She said it over and over as she sat on the floor of her shop, hoping it would sink in.

Nothing on the farm seemed willing to cooperate. Nobody was allowed off the grounds, not even for church. As hard as it was to skip worship, Gil felt a little distance was the safest thing for everybody. He tried to read a few Bible passages aloud in front of the fireplace Sunday morning, but no one paid attention. Unsettled by Mark's transgressions and bored by being on lockdown, the guys bickered constantly all weekend. A tractor broke, his computer froze twice and he was so distracted he deleted twelve files instead of backing them up. He wasn't hungry, the corrections department was breathing down his neck and he couldn't sleep.

By Sunday night, Gil was so frustrated and miserable. He walked into the living room after midnight to light a fire because he couldn't think of anything else to do.

He stopped in the doorway, frozen by the sight of Steven sitting on the floor in front of a single lit log in the fireplace.

And an open Bible.

"Don't take this away, God," Steven was saying quietly. "Mark screwed up somethin' fierce, and we're gonna lose Homestretch. I know I've been a jerk and all, but Gil keeps tellin' us You know what to do with jerks so I reckon You can fix this. You gotta fix this. I…um…well, I need this place. I can't go back. So I'm begging You, don't let a jerk like Mark and take Homestretch down. And don't let Gil give up—You and I both know he wants to. Just don't let him, okay?"

Gil stood still, stunned by what he heard.

Steven. The last guy on earth he'd think to come round.

What had he said to Emily? *Just when I think I finally found the batch that can't be turned around, one guy turns. That'll start the rest of them, and it works out.*

Gil left the room as silently as he'd entered it, leaving Steven to get acquainted with the God, who'd been waiting for him for years.

Alone in his room, Gil stared into the night sky for hours. Then, just before dawn, he drove to Emily's house.

Just to look at it. Because he needed to.

Emily was getting a bit annoyed. Her epiphany should have solved *something*. Given her at least a decent night's sleep or dawned a new day with more clarity.

It didn't. Nor did church. Sunday was a blur, and Sunday night had lagged on just as sleepless as the night before. She'd woken Monday still trapped inside a blizzard of emotions. Half of her was so weary she wanted to throw her arms around Gil and tell him nothing was beyond God's mercy and it would work out. But the other half was raw enough to walk away from him, from his complicated past and all his costly risks, and pretend they'd never gotten close.

The most excruciating thing of all was that she knew she could do neither.

She couldn't go back to him until she'd settled the matter of his record completely in her heart. She owed him that much. But even if God somehow managed to settle that issue, was that everything? What if more secrets lurked in his past? Could she handle it?

She looked up from her kitchen table and gazed out her windows, seeking the comfort from the sunrise.

He was there.

Gil was there, standing alone across the street. Oblivious to the weather, hands stuffed into his jean pockets, he stared at her house.

He looked as miserable as she felt.

She stared at him for a moment, kidding herself that he couldn't see into the kitchen and see her. Even with a great distance between them, their eyes locked. It was a full minute, maybe more, before she walked slowly to the front door and opened it.

Gil crossed the street, barely taking his eyes off her, and walked up to the gate. He came no farther, though, standing on the sidewalk, leaving her with her arms wrapped around her bathrobe, feeling the cold February air surrounding her in the doorway.

It was awful, standing there aching for a solution or the right thing to say and coming up empty.

"How are you?" His voice was low and unsteady.

The question was so ridiculous that it made the corner of her mouth turn up in a half smile. "Terrible."

"Me, too."

They held each other's gaze for a sore moment, before he looked down at the sidewalk. "I'd make it different if I could," Gil said finally. "But I can't."

"No." Emily could barely gulp the word out, her voice was so tight. It'd be so simple to pull him into the warmth of her kitchen, to tell a half-truth and say it'd all be okay, that she'd get over it. But it wasn't simple, she wasn't sure she'd get over it, and she wasn't sure it'd be okay. After a long moment she found the right question to ask. "Are you sorry?" It seemed a foolish, almost insulting question, but she needed to hear his answer. Maybe those words would be a place to start.

He didn't need to ask "about what." He didn't even need to speak an answer, actually. The pain and resignation in his eyes went miles beyond anything words could hold. "You've no idea," he said so quietly she barely heard him.

"I want it all to be okay," she said, her voice suddenly catching at the hopelessness of it all, "but…"

"But…" He wasn't cuing her to finish.

Not everything comes out in the wash. It was an odd thought, but then again it made a peculiar sense for the moment. *Some stains set in.*

Emily thought of her grandmother's old aprons, hung with reverence along one wall of her kitchen. They were thin and soft with age, but she kept them hanging there. She would trace her fingers around the stains after her grandmother died. She knew the stains—what they were, how they got there, the love and labor that made them. Those aprons wouldn't have been the same if the stains had come out.

But it wasn't the same thing.

She couldn't pretend it was the same thing.

He gave her one last look—a look that felt far too much like goodbye—before he turned and walked toward his truck. The emptiness of the sky after he left made Emily sit down and cry until she had no tears left.

Chapter Twenty-One

Emily struggled through her day at the shop, dimly aware of what she was doing. She put on the smiling face her customers expected, but mostly she played Edith Piaf and sat staring off into space for minutes at a time. She stared at the shiny new keys Janet had given her for the new locks, thinking they looked odd and unfamiliar on her keychain. Things were different now.

A few people mentioned how well she'd done at Character Day. She accepted their compliments, but it was bittersweet. She knew she'd done a good thing—an important thing—but it was hard to *feel* good about it. There had been such an aftermath. It felt almost like the months after Ash's death, when her only goal had been to endure the day, not enjoy it.

Sandy came in around closing time, and Emily came unhinged on the spot. They'd talked it through on Friday, but as tired as she was, it all came out all over again. Sandy just held her hand and listened, again. Sandy was always good at that. And when Emily finally calmed down and caught her breath, Sandy walked to the back of the store to put the kettle on for tea.

"I know everybody thinks it's the break-in, and it is, in a way, but it's mostly Gil," Emily said, trying not to sound downright devastated.

"I'm sorry you're so miserable. I was sort of hopin' you'd get an easy romance for your second time around. Then again, you always did like doing things the hard way. A man who's convinced himself he's unlovable is a mighty hard man to love." She stirred sugar into her tea and sat down at the little window table. "Do you love him?"

Sandy hadn't asked her that before. "I don't know. I thought maybe I was starting to. But now I don't know."

"Do you think he is the same kind of man as the one who wouldn't help Ash?"

"He was."

"I didn't ask you who you thought he *was*. I asked you who you think he *is*."

Emily leaned her head back against the wall. "I don't know who he is anymore. It's been days, Sandy, and I still don't know what to do, or how to fix this, or even if it can be fixed at all. I can't think of anything to solve this." She turned her head to catch Sandy's eyes. "Maybe that's what God had in mind all along."

"Well, I figured God was gonna have to go a long way to get your attention on that, but I didn't think He'd have to take it quite this far. So you're finally askin' God what to do instead of tellin' him what you're gonna do?"

Emily let out a thin, sorry laugh. "I figured that out, finally. But I thought my brilliant realization would help a bit more than it has. It's already Monday, and I'm still miserable."

"Emily Montague, queen of the solutions, doesn't have one anymore. And you expect to feel comfortable?"

"I want to be okay with all of it, but I can't push a button and make it happen. I'm not even sure it will happen."

Sandy placed a hand over Emily's. "This is big stuff. Important stuff. Things you and Gil have been carryin' around for years. It's not gonna sort itself out in a day or two. Or five. If you love him, I think you'll know it soon enough. In the meantime, I think the two of you have a whopping load of praying to do." She collected the empty tea mugs and stood up. "Tell you what—you stay home tomorrow and do whatever you feel will help. I'll watch the store for you—that new computer system of George's is drivin' me bananas anyway, and I wouldn't mind a day away from all that bionic nonsense. You go home and get quiet. You might just figure out how to listen if you do."

"Sandy, have I ever told you you're a Godsend?"

Sandy waved her hand as she headed back toward the little kitchen. "Not yet today, honey, but it's only five-thirty."

Emily pulled in a deep breath. "Just pray I figure out how to listen, okay? I'm just gonna keep asking 'What should I do?' until I get an answer."

Mac showed up.

Gil hadn't counted on that, and no one was more surprised when the front-gate intercom broadcast the familiar voice. Gil closed his eyes and gave a silent prayer of thanks as he hit the button opening Homestretch's front gate.

"You don't have to come," he said when he opened the door to Mac, who extended a friendly hand. "You're not on the town council and I ain't been particularly nice to you lately."

Mac managed a half grin. "You're never particularly nice to me. And how could I miss an emergency meeting of the Middleburg town council?" He put a hand on Gil's shoulder. "I'm comin'. So play nice, say thank you and get in the car."

"You're driving?"

"Yeah. That way I can stomp off anytime I want to and *you'll* have to find a ride home this time."

Gil started in on a comeback, then decided maybe this would be a good time to hush up and just accept a good friend's show of support. As a matter of act, they hardly talked at all the whole ride into town—Gil's head was a jumble of nerves, a tangle of all the things he'd planned to say. He'd spent the afternoon preparing his defenses, but all the reasons he'd gathered to keep Homestretch open seemed weak and useless now. He'd defended Homestretch in hundreds of ways over the years. Now, when it really mattered, with Steven's prayers ringing in his ears, he came up short.

The meeting room at the town hall was thick with tension. The undercurrent of mumbling, however, silenced the moment he entered. Emily did not look up. He was glad for that—he wasn't sure what it would do to him to look into her eyes right now, with so many people watching. The spectator chairs—usually half-empty—were all occupied and Mac had to stand in the back.

"I call this emergency meeting of the Middleburg Town Council to order," Howard said with all the gravity he could muster. "The single agenda item being recent events involving the West of Paris bath shop and Homestretch Farm."

"Honestly, Howard," Sandy cut in, "I don't see why this couldn't keep until next week. Don't you all think we need a little time to put this in perspective?"

"I don't need another minute," came a voice from the spectator seats. Gil turned to find Matt Lockwood staring him down. It didn't faze Gil. He'd expected Lockwood to jump on that position.

"Order, please!" Howard banged his gavel.

Sandy made a sour face and raised her hand as if she were in the third grade. She could have simply asked to be recognized—and really, things hardly ever got this formal at their other meetings. But Gil suspected Sandy was making a statement.

"The chair recognizes Mrs. Burnside."

Gil tried not to roll his eyes. In the full year he'd been on town council, even Howard had never had cause to use such formal language.

"I would like the record to show—" Sandy matched Howard's formality but filled her voice with sharp Southern bite "—that I object to the calling of this meeting."

Howard scowled over the top of his reading glasses. "On what grounds?"

Sandy huffed. "On account of we ain't had a lick of time to make any sense of this. What put the fire under you all? Normally we make decisions about as slow as molasses on this council, and now y'all want to turn around and slam something into gear without thinkin' it through just cuz you're uncomfortable? I thought I was servin' with better folks than that."

"You'd rather we put this on an ordinary agenda, beside road-widening and ATM machines?" another council member asked, her opinion obvious in her sharp tone of voice.

Mac's proposals. Gil hadn't thought of those until now.

All that preparation would go up in smoke. Mac's bid to work on those projects would be killed most likely, just because Gil had sponsored his ideas. Gil ventured a woeful glance at his friend, who simply nodded with an expression that made it clear he wouldn't go down without a fight.

"I have the right, as mayor, to call this meeting," Howard declared.

"You do," said Sandy. "You certainly do. But like any agenda item, this council has the right to table a vote if it so chooses. Am I right, Audrey?"

Audrey Lupine stopped taking minutes to flip open her big blue book of council rules and regulations, running her finger down a page until she looked up and said, "She does. I mean, we do. Have the right to vote to table any issue until a subsequent meeting, that is."

"I move we table the issue of Homestretch Farm until our next regular meeting," Sandy declared, staring right at Howard.

"Now hold your horses, people." Howard planted his hands on the table. "Let's make sure we do this right. And I'm afraid, Mr. Sorrent," Howard said, turning toward Gil, "we'll have to exclude you from this vote."

"I expected no less," Gil answered flatly. He was amazed they'd even let him in the room, given the way people seemed to be acting. Unfortunately, that left six votes, which could bring a stalemate and drag this out forever. He really didn't want this to last long; a lingering, drawn-out death would be more than he could take right now.

"Then you'll have to exclude me, too." It was Emily who spoke. Her voice was soft and slightly unsteady. She still didn't look at him. "I'm just as involved."

"I suppose you're right," Howard agreed.

It was obvious Sandy didn't like this idea. "Now wait a minute. Y'all can cross out their votes, but don't you think we ought to at least get their *opinions* on it all? Doesn't it matter to anyone if Gil and Emily *want* to decide things now or later?"

"It matters to me," Audrey said. "This ain't just a road or a building we're talking about. These are people. Neighbors."

"Crimes," another council member added.

Howard banged his gavel. "If y'all can't keep any order here…" he warned.

"Emily," Sandy asked, "what do you want to do?"

There was a short, quiet pause as Emily thought through her answer. Gil guessed she had no more solidified her stance than he had—the two of them were far too torn up to make any kind of sense on something so large. But he could see how she could call the whole thing to an end tonight. She knew he was thinking of shutting down Homestretch. She didn't know about Steven and his heart-wrenching prayer. She could call for the decision tonight, and she'd have every right to do so. Maybe some part of him even hoped she would—this was so awful, maybe it'd be better to just get it over with no matter what the outcome.

"I want it tabled." Emily spoke softly at first, but continued with more strength. "I think the issue should be tabled until we know more, until next week."

"Mr. Sorrent?"

Gil looked up. He hadn't even realized they'd ask his opinion, as well. It didn't take him long to formulate his answer. "I think Ms. Montague gets to call the shots here, Howard. If she wants it tabled, then I think it should be tabled." He'd endure another week on her behalf. It wouldn't kill him—it felt as if he was half-dead already anyway.

With only five remaining votes on the council, the matter was tabled by a 3–2 vote.

Like it or not, Mac and Gil would go down together at next week's meeting.

There was a moment—an aching, awful moment—when Gil caught Emily's eye. Like they had across her street the other morning. A storm of emotions passed between them in a single glance. Still, neither of them spoke.

Chapter Twenty-Two

Emily spent Wednesday quietly, taking Sandy's advice and staying away from the store to listen and heal. She cooked up a big batch of soup, took a long bath, and stared out the window waiting for some kind of peace. Finally, too restless to sit still another day, Emily went foraging through her basement for something to occupy her hands. On some shelves under her stairs, she found the books and ingredients from the time she'd dabbled in making her own soap.

Two of the necessary ingredients were upstairs: oil and water. She checked the expiration date on the third ingredient, a container of lye, and found it was still good. That's all that was really needed to make soap, and she had enough herbs, essential oils and scents in the house to make a batch of just about anything she wanted.

That was the chemical wonder of soap: oil and water—two things that normally can't combine well—are able to coexist with the addition of lye. It had always struck Emily as funny that these two uncombinable elements combined to make something as wonderful as soap.

And it was the lye that made it possible, also known as caustic soda or sodium hydroxide. It was so caustic that rubber gloves and a host of other protective clothing sat on the shelf beside the canister. Emily flipped through the recipe book, looking for whatever scent combination would appeal to her prickly mood. "Lye must be handled with care," the book cautioned. "It is volatile and dangerous."

"Sound like anyone we know?" Emily asked Othello, scooting his furry backside over as he tried to sit on the book. "Handle lye with respect, and soap-making is a completely safe process." Hadn't Gil said that treating those guys with respect was the key to turning them around? Respect—it turned them from unsafe hoodlums into responsible young men.

Water and oil couldn't become soap *without* lye. Certain recipes took as much as two hours of stirring in the lye-water to get the water and oil to combine in the right way. But no amount of stirring would make them combine without that dangerous element.

Which made her think. Maybe Gil couldn't have been the man he was now without having been the thug he was as a teen. Maybe he wouldn't have the success he had with those men if he hadn't had a similar past. Nothing made his crimes less criminal, just as lye never stopped being caustic. It was what you did with the dangerous element that made all the difference. Perhaps, with a little love and grace—with a lot of love and grace, actually—she could begin to see Gil's crime as the formative experience it was, despite her own personal history. Had not Moses committed murder? And God could still use him in ways Emily could never hope to match. And King David. His murder of Bathsheba's husband was downright malicious—one man killing another to get what he wanted. Hadn't God still used David? Both men were used by God because of who they became *after* their crimes. And she knew that if she tried to weaken the lye, to make it less dangerous, the results would be useless.

You had to wield a strong danger to get powerful results.

Soap, Emily realized, was mercy you could hold in your hand. She ticked down through the Edmundson's Fruits of the Spirit soaps in her head to find no mercy scent. There wasn't a mercy scent.

Yet.

Gil had stacked several feet of stone wall by lunchtime Tuesday. He'd toiled hard enough to work up a sweat despite the cold air, but he still felt like a walking tornado. Part of it was the inescapable fact that Homestretch's fate was hanging by a thread. Steven's prayer was right—Gil had been more than ready to throw in the towel. He, the tireless fighter, had been ready to give up. But now his fierce affection for the farm and its purpose made him nervous about the impending vote. Homestretch was all about second chances—it deserved a second chance of its own. It stung that it might not get one. He was helpless to change Homestretch's odds—he didn't have a vote. Nor did Emily.

And then there was everything with Emily.

Telling Emily had been the hard, right thing. He'd known Emily would run from his past, but that was his price to pay. She couldn't help but do so—he was what she'd spent years resenting: a person too cowardly to step forward and stop something horrible from happening. And neither of them could change what had already happened—the past is always set in stone.

The future was worse: He'd trained himself to be content with his work at Homestretch. Then he'd glimpsed a different future, and he'd allowed himself to ignore his past and wonder about a future with Emily. But now, because of that unchangeable past, he was helpless to build that future.

So he built the wall instead. *I hate this,* he prayed as he picked up a rock and scanned the wall for the right spot. *I don't deserve her but I need her. Make it go away, Lord. I can't stand this. I can't bear to close Homestretch now but I can't stand to stay.* He hoisted the rock into place and wedged it tight. He'd surely hit bottom again. Or sunk back down—that's really what it felt like.

Push off, Gil, go back down and push off.

Years ago, the man who'd set him on the right track, who'd introduced him to a radical Jesus whose mercy was bigger than his crimes, had made him do one thing: go back. On a bitterly cold night, they'd walked together to the street corner where Gil had hit rock bottom. "This is where you gotta push off from," the pastor had said. "You gotta start with your feet on the rock bottom you know." Gil had dreaded it, thinking it would be awful, but it was just a street corner. Ordinary, dirty, no different than thousands of others. He stood there, side by side with the burly, blessed youth pastor who would not leave him for hopeless, and claimed that spot. Claimed it for his future instead of surrendering it to his past. And it felt just like pushing off from the bottom. He stood there, shivering, promising himself he'd never go back to the person he was on that corner. Grabbing at his new life with both hands.

But he hadn't really done that.

Gil dropped the stone he was holding.

He hadn't done it at all.

He'd never really put that past behind him; he'd stopped now, when it mattered most. Mac was right: the best part of his new life was slipping through his fingers. Actually, he was pushing it away like a fool, like some kind of penance he'd condemned himself to pay forever. What was Jesus if not big enough to make a new man out of the skinny, stupid kid who wouldn't do the hard, right thing all those years ago?

How could he tell these guys Christ could transform their lives if he refused to let Him transform his own?

It was time to take his Redeemer at His word.

Gil left the wall and went to his office. He threw his cell phone and PDA onto the desk, walked past all the computers and printers and screens—the technology that had found him answers in the past—and picked up a plain old pencil and notepad. He headed back outside and down the front drive, barely waiting for the gates to slide open before he ducked through them to stand on the gravel shoulder.

The side of the road by the Homestretch gate. Because that was the place to push off from the bottom again.

Like the last time, the spot looked dull and ordinary. Patches of slush dotted brown winter grass and gravel. A side of the road like a thousand others. It offered no big revelations just by standing on it. So, he set about doing what the pastor had had him do all those years ago. He hiked himself up to sit on the stone wall of the gate and pulled the notepad from his coat pocket. Snagging the pencil from behind his ear, he wrote WHAT I KNOW in capital letters across the top of his page. The pastor had said what you know at the bottom is the truest knowledge of all.

Gil put a fat number 1 on the first line and waited for his brain to fill it in.

After ten minutes, he scribbled "I feel lousy." Not exactly the self-actualization he was hoping for, but honesty was always a good place to start.

2. I want her in my life.

Even though some part of him insisted she didn't belong there, a bigger part of him refused to let her go. Wanted what she did to him, how she made him feel and think.

3. She has to know about my past.

He'd always known that on some level, even if he tried to convince himself otherwise. But *why* did she have to know? The other women—there'd only been a few—hadn't had to know. He'd had women pressure him to talk about his past, but he'd always resisted. Even flat-out refused. So why now, when the information did such whopping damage, did he insist on revealing it?

He knew why. He'd always known why.

4. I love her.

Emily was right: he'd held back, keeping his past as a secret, as the trump card to end it all when she got too close. Because he was terrified of her. Emily meant something real to him—something deep that he'd convinced himself he couldn't have and didn't deserve.

But I want it now, Lord. I want her in my life. I want to be the man I am when I'm with her.

Here, now, was he any different than any of his guys? Any of the dozens of men he'd helped? Without even re-

alizing it, he'd decided he wasn't capable of turning his life
around. Convinced himself that it was too hard, that the
world—or what it just Emily?—was too unwilling to grant
him a second chance. Each man on the farm received a
small, wooden token to carry in his pocket. Gil had stopped
carrying his. At the time, he'd convinced himself it was just
laziness, but now he realized it might have been something
bigger. He wrote the saying that was on the token:

5. God values the man I am.

I'd stopped believing that, didn't I, Lord? Gil shut his
eyes and prayed. *Worked hard so You'd be impressed by
what I do, but forgot You value who I am. How'd I get so
far off track while settin' other people on theirs?*

He returned to the notepad.

6. Emily…

Gil didn't know how to finish that. Emily…could love
me? Emily…might love me? Emily…wants to love me?
Each time he came up with an option, Gil realized he didn't
have any way of knowing those things, nor did he have any
control over them.

*Okay, Lord, I need a little help here. What's within my
control that I can know?*

It came to him:

6. Emily is worth fighting for. Now.

He sprinted up the front drive and threw himself into the
truck before he could talk himself out of it. The tires spat

gravel as he roared out of the Homestretch gates, heading for town. He knew her store closed at five, and it was already twenty till. The truck couldn't go fast enough. When he got stuck behind some farm machinery, he was crazed with frustration. "You gonna let it all go to pieces now?" he roared while he banged his hands on the steering wheel. "Come on, God, cut a guy a break here. I'm finally gettin' this right."

Chapter Twenty-Three

The batch of soap had gone horribly wrong.

Emily stared at the unimpressive little rectangle. Normally, her soaps looked artisan and handmade. But this batch looked more like something scraped off the bottom of a pot. The cinnamon and orange scents she'd put in—always tricky to get a masculine scent rather than anything floral—had gone a little wrong, and the bar smelled like overripe cider. It had an orangey-brown tinge that couldn't really be called attractive. She stepped back and cocked her head to one side, declaring it one of her least successful attempts at soap-making. A casual observer might easily mistake it for a preschool art project.

But she loved it. The fact that she'd only had enough mixture left to form two bars because she'd slipped and dropped the pot only added to the charm.

Just two bars. Like the two bars that started everything. The imperfection fit, somehow. She held her bar up to Othello, deciding that lopsided rectangles were artistic. "We're shooting for feeling here, not fancy." Othello blinked, stretched out his head to give it an inquisitive sniff, and promptly dismissed her creation as nothing he found worthy of his attention. "Everyone's a critic," she said as she reached for some yellow paper.

Emily wasn't sure if she could ever explain to Gil how the concept of lye being necessary to make soap helped her come to terms with everything. Even when she said it out loud to Othello it sounded ridiculous.

"Nobody needs to get it but me and God," Emily declared to the empty kitchen.

Carefully, she copied down the long verse from 1 Timothy onto the paper. "I was shown mercy so that in me, the worst of sinners, Christ Jesus might display his unlimited patience as an example for those who would believe on him and receive eternal life." It had taken her some time to decide on the passage, but she'd known it was right. She got a warm feeling in her chest when she thought about her handwriting nestled snug up against the soap.

Ms. Montague's Mercy Soap had its first customer.

Well, Ms. Montague's Mercy Soap had only two customers. This particular scent would be a limited edition, two-of-a-kind production.

"Othello, I need to go pay a visit to Gil. He doesn't know it yet, but he needs one more bar of soap in his life." She gave Othello a kiss on the top of his fuzzy head and grabbed her car keys.

Gil's red truck pulled into the parking space in front of West of Paris just as Sandy Burnside was locking up the front door. He spilled out of the truck, leaving it running.

"Where is she?"

Sandy looked at him. She knew everything, he could tell by the way she looked at him. "Who?"

"Sandy…"

Sandy tucked the shop keys into that monstrous handbag of hers and leaned back against the door. Hang her, she knew everything that was going on, but she looked as if she was having a pleasant Sunday chat. "Do you love her?" she said calmly.

Gil rolled his eyes. "What?"

"You heard me."

"Sandy, don't you think I ought to be havin' that conversation with *Emily?*"

"She ain't here. I am. Now I know where she is and you don't, so unless you want to find out who's the more stubborn here—and trust me, it's a draw—answer the question."

"Sandy…" It was turning into a growl with every repetition.

She crossed her arms over her chest and casually inspected a fingernail. "I ain't got nowhere to be, hon. Take your time."

Middleburg was full of meddling crazy people. He stalked the sidewalk for a moment, thinking that this was insane. This wasn't a declaration for the middle of town. Sandy had no business knowing. He could find Emily himself if he had to—it's not as if he didn't know where she lived.

Unless she'd gone somewhere. He thought she'd never leave the shop, but maybe, if she was in pain, she *would* go off somewhere. Ask Sandy to mind the shop. He didn't think he could stand another hour, let alone days, without talking to Emily.

"Fine." He threw up his hands. "You win. I love her. I've fallen for her completely, like some kind of lovesick idiot. Now will you please tell me where she is before I—"

She held up one hand. "Now, now, no need to get all prickly on me, I just needed to make sure we had our priorities in order." She smiled warmly and he tamped down the urge to yell at her. "She's at home."

"You knew she was home the whole time and—" Gil decided he didn't have a polite way to finish that sentence. He threw himself back into the truck and pulled out of the parking space with only enough time to hear Sandy call, "You're welcome," while waving from the sidewalk.

It was a two-minute drive to Emily's house. In his state of mind, he could have run it in one.

Her VW wasn't out front. That doesn't really mean anything, he told himself as he threw open the little white gate and took her front stairs in a single lunge. He banged on the door. "Emily!" A fat orange cat poked its head through the living-room window curtains and blinked at him, but no one answered the door.

"What do you mean she's not home?" Gil moaned into the air. "Sandy said she was home. She's not home. How can she not be home?" The cat blinked again and settled onto the top of the couch back, as if this might make for entertaining viewing. "Where is she?" he asked the cat through the window, then practically slapped his head for the stupidity of it all. "Cats. I'm asking cats."

Where is she? Where would she have gone? Lord, don't do this to me. Don't make me wait for her now. He stood on Emily's tiny front porch for ten minutes, helpless and frustrated beyond belief.

There was nothing to be done.

At first he thought he'd just camp out on her steps until she came home. She'd come back from wherever she was mending her wounds, she'd find him here and they'd start the long process of talking it out.

He realized, picturing that homecoming, that he hadn't even kissed her yet. He sank down onto the porch steps, astounded.

How could he possibly be in love with someone he hadn't even kissed yet? It was like some sort of sick fairy tale where the frail princess and the swaggering prince sigh at each other from afar. *I'm not that kind of hero,* he almost laughed to himself. *I really am in over my head here. How about a little help here, Lord? Big ol' hunk of divine guidance coming down out of the sky to tell me what to do?*

This had gone way too fast. Maybe they did need time. Maybe they needed to wait a bit. *Wait? Now? You remember, Lord, how bad I am at waiting?*

He'd set out in his truck determined to fix everything, to make it all better. He drove home without a clue as to what came next.

Chapter Twenty-Four

The sun was setting, and it was getting cold. Ethan had answered the gate buzzer, but told Emily Gil wasn't there. He'd gone off "in a supreme huff," Ethan said, leaving his cell phone and PDA on his desk and tearing off in his truck without a word to anyone. Ethan invited her in to wait in the house, but Emily declined. It felt better, somehow, to stay out here at the gate.

She was just about to give up when she caught sight of the red truck coming over the hill. Her heart slammed around in her chest as he drove closer. *Oh, God, make this all right between us. I'll settle for whatever You decide, but You know how much he means to me now. I won't ask, because You already know. I'll try and trust You, really I will.*

She couldn't see Gil's face behind the windshield. She had no idea what his mood was as he pulled the truck up against the gate just as he'd done before. Emily held her breath as she got out of her car.

It was an ordinary front gate on a dusky February night. Nothing romantic or significant, just a muddy roadside in front of a place she'd come to hold dear. Taking a deep breath, Emily pulled off her hat and said, "Gil?"

He got out of the truck slowly, with the most unreadable expression on his face. Emily wrapped her hand around the soap in her pocket and tried to breathe.

"You weren't home," he said.

"You went looking for me?" She dared to hope that was a good thing. When they'd last stood at this gate, he'd sounded as if he never wanted to see her again. "Gil…"

He walked straight to her. "I'm sorry I waited to tell you. You were right. I—I was scared of this. I'm sorry."

Emily shook her head. "I'm sorry I held all that against you. I hadn't even realized how unforgiving I still was. When I made the speech, I thought I'd come through it all and then it all came back when you told me and…" She trailed off. "I can't make any sense. I think it will be a long time before any of this makes sense."

He reached out to her, his rough hands tracing one strand of her hair as it fell against her cheek. "I want to try to make sense of this. More than anything. Do you believe that?"

She'd told herself they would take it slow. Take it one careful step at a time. But when he touched her, when the setting sun caught the surprising tenderness in his eyes, none of that mattered. She threw herself into his arms so hard he stumbled back a bit. He laughed as he righted the two of them, a bright warm laugh she'd never heard from him.

And then he kissed her. Fierce and desperate and without anything held back. She felt the last of the thick wall he'd built around himself come down in her arms and knew this was what God had intended all along. When he pulled away to look into her eyes, it was like a different man staring at her. The one she'd only seen glimpses of before, the one hiding behind the wall.

Sandy's question had been right. Was this man the same man as the one who'd left Ash back on that street corner? No. This man in front of her had been someone like that, long ago, but now all things had been made new. Her own heart included.

"I've…um…brought you something," she stammered, suddenly finding it hard to catch her breath. "I made this for you."

Gil took the little rectangle in yellow paper from her hand, his head cocked to one side in surprise. "Is that what I think it is?"

"Not exactly."

He peered at the handwritten wrapper. "Ms. Montague's Mercy Soap." He turned it over in his hand, looking at it.

"I've made soap before," she started, diving into an explanation she could only hope would make sense. "I don't know why I started up again today, but I was so confused, and it was the only thing that kept coming to me when I prayed. So I made a batch this morning."

Gil hoisted himself up onto the stone wall and offered his free hand pull her up with him. He pulled her up easily, then wrapped his arm around her as they sat on the stones in the fading light. "You see," she said, taking the soap from his hand and holding it up for him so he wouldn't have to take his wonderfully strong arm from around her, "soap's got three things in it. The first two aren't supposed to mix— oil and water. I found that, well, sort of metaphorical."

He grabbed the hand holding the soap and kissed it, mitten and all. "I get what you mean."

"But you *can* get them to mix. It takes a third element. If you don't use it, the oil and water won't mix and it won't work. And that's lye."

"Lye? Drain cleaner?"

"Well, the same chemical. It's caustic and dangerous and they say—oddly enough—that the trick is to treat it with respect. Sound familiar?"

"I think I follow you." The wide, warm smile had yet to leave his face.

"At first, I thought of your past as the dangerous part of you. The part that could hurt me. But it's the part of you that makes you able to do what you do. It's valuable even though it's dangerous—just like the lye. And the same with me. My past is hard for you, but it's part of who I am, so it's the same. We both have corrosive things in our lives, but we can choose to make them work for us, to help us mix when it seems like we shouldn't."

"So I have to ask: What's mercy smell like?"

"Not as good as I'd hoped," Emily admitted, laughing, feeling relief as the sorrow of the past few days simply slipped away. "It should be Ms. Montague's Mistake Soap."

"Nah," he said, looking up at her with a glint that made her stomach flip. "I like the mercy part." He lifted his arm from around her and worked the wrapper off. He knew, as she knew he would, to look inside, even though he had to squint in the dusk. "I was shown mercy so that in me, the worst of sinners, Christ Jesus might display his unlimited patience as an—" his voice caught a bit, and she knew she'd chosen the right verse "—as an example for those who would believe on him and receive eternal life."

"That's you. That's what happened to Ash." She touched

the wrapper in his hand. "But I've realized now, everything is redeemable if you believe in mercy."

"It's the whole point of Homestretch Farm, but I've never gotten it, really," Gil said. "I've been telling the guys that for years, never realizing that I wouldn't let it apply to me. And then you…"

He couldn't speak for a moment. Emily guessed he had a lump in his throat as large as the lump in hers.

"We've got to fight for it," Emily said, looking up into his eyes. "Now that I get what this place is all about, now that I know what I know, I can't bear the thought of them voting to close Homestretch."

Gil let his head lean against hers. "I know."

"I'll fight it. We'll fight it. We'll find a way to make them see. They can't close it because of Mark—it's the guys like Mark that need Homestretch to stay open. There's got to be a way to make them see it. God will show us the solution, and we can be strong if we're together."

Gil nodded, brushing his hand against her cheek. "And we *are* together. You and I." His eyes weren't dark at all now, just rich and deep and warm.

After another incredibly tender kiss, he held the bar closer and gave it a sniff.

"Whoa, there," he choked, his eyes watering. "You've got enthusiasm, I'll give you that much." He laughed, and she laughed, and the world righted itself into someplace wonderful where anything could happen. Gil reached out and tucked a strand of hair behind her ear, letting his hand linger on her cheek. He closed his eyes for a second, and he knew he was letting the moment sink in, savoring it. "I am in love with you. You know that."

"Yes." She let her face tilt into the warmth of his hand.

"And I'm in love with you, Gil."

His arms wrapped around her and pulled her tight, holding her as if she'd been gone for years. In a way, she had.

"Come on inside."

Epilogue

September was unusually hot that year. The cluster of tough-looking young men fidgeted in their chairs, looking as if they'd rather be anywhere but in the Homestretch Farm living room.

Emily took a few snapshots for her new scrapbook. These would look nice next to the clippings about the town council voting to keep Homestretch open. And the shots of Middleburg's two new artfully mounted ATM machines. It had been a big year. She made sure to get a really good picture of Paulo, even though he looked as if his shirt was making him itch. Sandy had provided him with a nice shirt and pants for job interviews—she had done that for all the "graduating" men—and Paulo looked handsome, if a bit out of his element.

Gil leaned over Emily's shoulder. "You think he can pull it off?" he whispered.

Emily nodded, then caught Paulo's eye as she took one more photo and gave him a thumbs-up.

"You guys don't know what you're in for here," Paulo

began, looking around the room. "I didn't. And I looked just like you, and I bet I felt just like you, last year. I was pretty sure this was just another of those stupid programs. But it ain't."

The newbies traded glances with each other, suspicious. Paulo cleared his throat nervously. Gil nodded and motioned for him to continue. Emily felt Gil's hand tighten around hers.

"The way I figure it, you got two choices. You can take this chance, or blow it. My friend Steve, he took it. He's my roommate now, and he's got a serious job making good money. We live in Lexington, and next year I'll probably have enough money saved up to get a car. Always wanted a car. I'm takin' a few classes, I got an okay job, but Steve? He's gonna make it. Big. He's really smart that way. One of you guys could be a Steve, and you probably don't even know it yet.

"My other friend, Mark? He blew his chance here, blew his parole, and he's back where he started. One of you guys could be Mark, too, and you won't know it until that chance comes and you gotta figure out if you're gonna take it. And it'll come. Count on it. You gotta decide how you're gonna go from here. Mr. Sorrent's cool, even if he does yell and work your butt off." Paulo looked over to Gil. "You can trust him."

Let them hear it, Emily prayed as Paulo finished his speech. She was happy that Paulo had been invited to welcome the new guys when Steve couldn't make it because of work. Paulo had a gift for words, even if he was a little rough around the edges still. *Let Paulo get through to them. Oh, they all look so young and lost. Did Paulo really look like that last year?*

* * *

As the sun went down and Ethan was busy getting everyone settled into their bunks, Gil saddled up Lady Macbeth and took Emily out to the cathedral. Slanted golden sun poked through the trees as the hills took on shades of purple and gray. It was still hot, but a quiet ease had swept over the fading day.

Emily watched Gil spread out a blanket on the grass. She sat down beside him, tucked under his arm, and they watched the light settle over the rolling hills.

"A new batch." He sighed. "I've never been so thankful to have another new batch."

"Do they always look so tough?" Emily asked, remembering the four earrings on one of them.

"Nah, last year's batch looked far tougher. These guys are cupcakes."

She poked him, knowing he was teasing. He'd become a great teaser over the summer, suddenly sprouting a sense of humor no one ever knew he had.

"I got one more secret," he said as he pulled her close and kissed the top of her head. Emily loved when he did that. Such a tender gesture from a man so large and strong.

"I don't know that I can take another secret." She wasn't entirely kidding.

"It's kinda necessary to reveal this one." Oh, that didn't sound good. What on Earth did he have to reveal this time?

He shifted in the grass and cleared his throat.

Emily began to get nervous. He was serious. He looked disturbingly uncomfortable.

"My…well…the truth is…my full name is…Gilbert."

Emily's eyes flew wide open. She tried to stifle a chuckle, but to no avail. Gilbert? Who put *that* name on *this* man? It'd be hard to come up with a less-fitting moniker. "Gilbert? Seriously?"

Gil turned eight shades of red. "I would not kid about that. Congratulations, you're one of about three people who know. Guard that secret with your life. And just make sure you say it softly when you have to."

Emily looked at him. "When I have to? When would I have to?"

Gil threw her a sideways glance. "You have to say my full legal name when you say 'I, Emily, take you…' well, you know…the whole lawfully wedded husband part."

Leave it to Gil Sorrent to come up with the world's first ever information-on-a-need-to-know-basis proposal. That was Gil, still occasionally telling her what to do. In this case, however, she didn't mind.

"Yes. That thing you didn't quite ask me just now? My answer is yes."

He beamed. "I think there's only one spot in the world for our honeymoon, don't you? Do you like the sound of a honeymoon in Paris? Paris, *France?*"

She beamed right back. There were only two words to fit the moment: "I do!"

* * * * *

Dear Reader,

Often we think we've got our life worked out. We've got a plan, we've asked God to bless it, and we're set to go. That's usually when God steps in and asks us to go in a completely different direction. Those directions—the ones we call "detours"—are faith's proving ground, where we learn that God's vision is different from our own and that calling Him "Lord" often means following where we cannot see. And, if you're like me, when I *think* I'm getting better at it, I discover I'm not. No fun.

Emily and Gil learn the same lesson just "sudsier." We plan our life in one direction like Emily, or confine our life in one direction like Gil. Either one refutes God's spectacular provision. I hope Emily and Gil's story reminds you that God has no confines and often has higher plans.

Blessings to each of you. Write me anytime at www.alliepleiter.com or P.O. Box 7026, Villa Park, Il 60181.

QUESTIONS FOR DISCUSSION

1. Read the list of fruits of the spirit given in Galatians 5:22-23. Which ones are your strengths? Which are your weaknesses?

2. If you could open a shop of any kind anywhere in the world (with a guarantee of success), what and where would it be? Does the answer tell you anything surprising about yourself?

3. What would you do in Emily's place when faced with the dilemma of the Pirate Soap?

4. A long hot bath is one way to destress. What's yours? How does it differ from those of your friends or family?

5. What would you consider your primary sense? Are you a scent person, a taste person, or a sight person? How does that impact your surroundings? Your worship?

6. Are you a forward-looking gadget guru or a vintage-loving history buff? What about your friends? Do those styles clash or do they meld in how you interact?

7. When has a friend nudged you to do something hard, as Sandy does in asking Emily to make the speech? How did you grow from it? Were you glad you did it?

8. Think about Edmund Burke's statement, "The only thing necessary for evil to triumph is for good men to

do nothing." Do you agree? Where has that idea surfaced in your life?

9. Has someone in your life disappointed you as Mark disappoints Gil? How can we recover from such blows? What are the lasting effects?

10. Did you grow up in a small town like Middleburg? If not, do you wish you had? What's the benefit of that kind of community? What's the downside of it?

11. Why was it so hard for Gil to forgive himself? What makes us deny ourselves full redemption, even as Christians? What do we lose in that denial?

12. Do you know a faithfully serving "Audrey" who could use some recognition? What can you do to show him/her that their service is valued?

13. Do you have anything like Homestretch Farm in your community? If yes, how do you feel about it? If no, how would you feel about a Homestretch Farm coming to your community?

*Turn the page for a sneak preview of
the next book in Allie Pleiter's
Kentucky Corners Series,*
BLUEGRASS COURTSHIP

Hollywood just invaded the paint aisle. Janet Bishop stood at the back of her hardware store and watched gel-haired, too-tanned Drew Downing strut past the exterior semigloss.

No semigloss here. This guy was the human definition of high-gloss. Three silver lock nuts on a leather strip around his neck. Trendy expensive sneakers. Gleaming teeth. Hundred-dollar jeans with rips in both knees. Better suited for a Beverly Hills café than a Kentucky hardware store. His only saving grace was that he did not have a television camera in tow.

Yet.

And to think that a mere minute ago she was hanging a collection of her charming birdhouses as a window display, her chest filling with satisfaction at the artistic little birdhouses she made in a variety of architectural styles.

And then her window had filled with an ominous shadow. Or, more precisely, bright green, for that was the color of the huge bus blocking her sunlight. Trouble had arrived in an emerald behemoth that hissed to a stop smack-dab in front of Bishop Hardware.

Buses full of tourists were fairly normal in Middleburg, Kentucky. It was a charming, rustic—okay, sometimes a little too rustic—town in the middle of horse country. This thing, however, was more like a rolling subdivision than your average charter bus. When Howard Epson came huffing down the street after this bus, things got even more interesting. Howard was Middleburg's hefty town mayor, and never ran for anything...except office. Anything that drove Howard to exertion was news indeed.

In reality, it wasn't Howard's trot that heralded disaster. It was the large white letters, the white foot-high type that spelled out MISSIONNOVATION.

The *Missionnovation* TV program. Janet didn't refer to them as "Hollywood's Heavenly Hardware Hypsters" for nothing.

"Howard Epson," Janet muttered under her breath as the sea of awestruck faces followed Drew Dawson down the long aisle toward her, "I will never vote for you again as long as I live." This was Howard's doing. He'd submitted Middleburg to the television show's heart-tugging charity hotline and done the unthinkable: put Middleburg Community Church up for a Missionnovation Ministry Makeover.

And it was here. Now. Oozing charisma and energy all over the store. *I'm sure they couldn't resist,* Janet thought as she crossed her arms over the bib of her overalls. It was perfect drama-fodder for those types: tiny town church preschool gets smashed by hundred-year-old tree in summer storm. Cherub-faced toddlers forced to learn primary colors in the YMCA gym because their preschool had been destroyed. Bake sales to buy new roofs and spaghetti dinner to fund drywall.

"My stars!" came a woman's awestruck squeal from

over by the gardening supplies. "It's those *Missionnovation* folks! From TV! Here! Edna, look! It's *him*."

Downing chose that exact moment to spread his arms wide and yelled his trademark, "Well, God bless ya and hello, Middleburg!" Janet was not feeling particularly blessed at that moment. Besieged was more like it. She'd done her share of groaning over Drew Downing's slippery charm as he led his team through "miraculous" church renovations on Thursday nights. Mocking him on television was one thing. Having him invade the town with his camera-poking posse of dynamic do-gooders was quite another.

Not that Janet begrudged fixing the church and pre-school. She'd already donated as much material to the cause as her budget would allow, and had even spent two Saturdays last month helping to tarp over the roof's giant hole. It was that MCC's crisis had just officially become a spectacle. A televised spectacle.

Eight seconds.

Sometimes five, but never more than eight.

Drew Downing knew the world divided itself up into people who loved what he did, and people who hated it. After three seasons of *Missionnovation,* Drew could size up on which side of that very thing line any one person stood. Always in under eight seconds.

He didn't need the last five. It only took three seconds to tell Bishop Hardware would be no ally to his cause. "Hostiles," his producer Charlie Buchanan called them. Sometimes you could win 'em over, most times, no matter what you did, they were just sure you had an angle and an agenda. If the hostiles couldn't find an angle, they never took it to mean you just might not have one, it only meant you were slicker than they thought and hid it very well. A no-win situation.

And those dark eyebrows on the pretty face of that woman standing with her feet apart at the end of the paint aisle? Well, they had No Win written in giant, neon letters.

"How may I help you?"

Wow, Drew thought, I didn't know you could make "How may I help you" sound like "Get out of this store right now." It shouldn't actually be possible. Then again, by the look on her face, maybe it was.

"Well, that's just it," Drew said, turning his gaze to the excited crowd that had pooled into the store behind him. "I'm here to ask you the same thing."

I'll bet, the woman' scowl seemed to say. Drew could be in a sea of people thrilled to meet him, and the only thing that would hold his focus was the one person who looked sure he was on the take. Charlie was always giving him a hard time about his obsession to win over the hostiles.

It was a hard habit to shake when you were once one of those skeptics yourself.

"Mr. Downing, we sure are glad to see you and your team here." A chubby older man Drew recognized as the mayor from the application video grabbed his hand and shook it vigorously. "I never dreamed when I sent in the application—"

"Don't say that," Drew stopped him, clasping one of the man's shoulders. "You did dream. That's why you asked for our help. And I'm glad you did. That means you must be Mayor Epson."

"I am," he beamed. A few of the locals patted him on the back. This part never got old. Watching the person who'd sent in the application get to be a hero. That application process was a lot of work. It took passion and persistence to make it as a *Missionnovation* target project. Getting to tell that person that their persistence had paid off and their dream project would be realized, well, that was the high-octane fuel that enabled Drew to pull as many all-nighters as he did.

"Howard Epson, your life's about to change. Your town's about to get a shot in the arm like only *Missionnovations* can deliver. Are you up for it?'

These folks watched television. They knew what to do when Drew Downing asked, "Are you up for it?" The tiny crowd yelled "You Betcha!" so loudly it echoed throughout the store. Two teenaged girls grabbed a sheet of paint chip samples off the display next to them and held it out to Drew, asking for his autograph. Out of the corner of his eye, Drew caught the lady in the overalls rolling her eyes.

"There'll be plenty of time for that kind of stuff later, gals," Drew said to the dreamy-eyed pair as he held out both elbows. "How's about you pretty ladies escort me and my crew over to the church so we can take a look? We got a ton of work ahead of us and daylight's burning."

They giggled as Drew made a show of sauntering up the aisle toward the exit. "I do love my job," he said, acting all sheepish even though the girls couldn't be more than fourteen. "It's a blessing every day." He stopped, flashing his gaze back and forth between the girls. "Wait a minute. You girls think you could convince a horde of your male admirers to come on over tomorrow and lend a little muscle? We need all the hands we can get on demolition day."

The girls, sweet girls but hardly beauties, flushed and giggled. If they were in charge of bringing teens onto the set, they'd be the most popular girls in school tomorrow. Drew loved to use his status to light up someone on the sidelines.

"I suppose we can find a few friends," they cooed.

"Then I'll put you in charge of strapping young volunteers. You go see Alice in the bus and she'll get you all set up with a box of T-shirts to give out as you sign folks up, okay?"

"Sure!" said the wide-eyed pair as they bubbled up the aisles toward Alice, who'd be waiting in the bus as always.

"Mayor Epson, I guess you'll need to lead the way."

"I'd be delighted! Right this way."

Drew turned back to the woman, who hadn't moved from her spot at the end of the paint aisle. He noticed, for the first time, that she wore a Bishop Hardware nametag, and that the name was Janet Bishop. Owner? Daughter of the owner? Wife of the owner? It was too soon to say. "We'll be back later with a mighty long list," he said, pointing right at her.

She looked unconvinced.

Why do they always look unconvinced?

Love Inspired

Cheerful army nurse
Madeline Bright quickly
becomes the darling of
Prairie Springs, Texas.
And if ex-pilot
Jake Hopkins isn't
careful, she might just
conquer his heart. Being
around Maddie brings
back too many painful
memories for Jake.
Can he allow her to be
a part of his life?

Look for

At His Command

by

Brenda Coulter

HOMECOMING ★ HEROES ★

*Saving children and
finding love deep in
the heart of Texas*

*Available September wherever books are sold,
including most bookstores, supermarkets,
drugstores and discount stores.*

www.SteepleHill.com

Love Inspired

Only one person knows why Kat Thatcher left her Oklahoma hometown ten years ago. That person is Seth Washington. And now that she's back, he's only too available to talk about the past. Seth insists the Lord is on their side and always was. But will that be enough for love?

Look for

A Time To Heal
by
Linda Goodnight

Available September wherever books are sold, including most bookstores, supermarkets, drugstores and discount stores.

Love Inspired.
HISTORICAL
INSPIRATIONAL HISTORICAL ROMANCE

Adelaide Crum longs for a family, but the closed-minded town elders refuse to entrust even the most desperate orphan to a woman alone. Newspaperman Charles Graves promises to stand by her, despite his embittered heart. Adelaide's gentle soul soon makes him wonder if he can overcome his bitter past, and somehow find the courage to love....

Look for

Courting Miss Adelaide
by
JANET DEAN

Steeple
Hill®

LIH82796

REQUEST YOUR FREE BOOKS!

2 FREE INSPIRATIONAL NOVELS
PLUS 2
FREE
MYSTERY GIFTS

YES! Please send me 2 FREE Love Inspired® novels and my 2 FREE mystery gifts (gifts are worth about $10). After receiving them, if I don't wish to receive any more books, I can return the shipping statement marked "cancel". If I don't cancel, I will receive 4 brand-new novels every month and be billed just $4.24 per book in the U.S. or $4.74 per book in Canada, plus 25¢ shipping and handling per book and applicable taxes, if any*. That's a savings of over 20% off the cover price! I understand that accepting the 2 free books and gifts places me under no obligation to buy anything. I can always return a shipment and cancel at any time. Even if I never buy another book, the two free books and gifts are mine to keep forever.

113 IDN ERXA   313 IDN ERWX

Name _____ (PLEASE PRINT) _____

Address _____ Apt. # _____

City _____ State/Prov. _____ Zip/Postal Code _____

Signature (if under 18, a parent or guardian must sign)

Order online at www.LoveInspiredBooks.com

Or mail to Steeple Hill Reader Service:
IN U.S.A.: P.O. Box 1867, Buffalo, NY 14240-1867
IN CANADA: P.O. Box 609, Fort Erie, Ontario L2A 5X3

Not valid to current subscribers of Love Inspired books.

**Want to try two free books from another series?
Call 1-800-873-8635 or visit www.morefreebooks.com**

* Terms and prices subject to change without notice. N.Y. residents add applicable sales tax. Canadian residents will be charged applicable provincial taxes and GST. Offer not valid in Quebec. This offer is limited to one order per household. All orders subject to approval. Credit or debit balances in a customer's account(s) may be offset by any other outstanding balance owed by or to the customer. Please allow 4 to 6 weeks for delivery. Offer available while quantities last.

Your Privacy: Steeple Hill Books is committed to protecting your privacy. Our Privacy Policy is available online at www.SteepleHill.com or upon request from the Reader Service. From time to time we make our lists of customers available to reputable third parties who may have a product or service of interest to you. If you would prefer we not share your name and address, please check here. ☐

LIREG08R